Nick + Kathy,
Merry Chr
I hope you enjoy this book

Glen

HOSEA AND GOMER

A Love Story

By
Glen H. Von Wald

PublishAmerica
Baltimore

Softcover 9781462660414
PUBLISHED BY PUBLISHAMERICA, LLLP
www.publishamerica.com
Baltimore

Printed in the United States of America

As all my other writings have been,
This book is dedicated to the memory of my wife,
CAROLEEN L. VON WALD

INTRODUCTION

The experience of the prophet, Hosea, was unique among all the Hebrew prophets of the Bible. In addition to his responsibility of speaking the word of God, his life was to be used as an object lesson to the people of Israel. His life was to be a living demonstration of the Love of God. This demonstration was embarrassing and painful to him. His wife abandoned him and his family became dysfunctional in pining over her loss. He was a prophet with a broken heart, representing a God who suffered the same.

Hosea was commanded by God to love and marry a woman who was a prostitute. He married just such a woman. Her name was Gomer and from all scriptural evidence we can be sure that he did love her dearly. She lived with him for a number of years and bore him three children. Then for some reason, she leaves her husband and children and returns to a life as a prostitute. What would prompt her to do this? What was she thinking at the time? Whatever the reason was, she became a prostitute all over again.

A number of years after Gomer deserted him, Hosea was passing by a market where they were selling slaves. Out of the corner of his eye, he thought he recognized one of the female slaves being sold. As he took a closer look, he recognized his estranged wife, Gomer. As she got older, they didn't want her for a prostitute anymore. So they sold her as a slave. As he gazed upon her, Hosea felt the love that he had always had for her become even stronger than it ever was before. He had to do something.

Excusing himself from the party of friends that he was with, he started home to get his money so he could buy Gomer. His friends protested, telling his that she wasn't worth buying. She had shamed him. She made her bed, let her lie in it. She didn't deserve rescuing. However, Hosea was not acting on what she had done or what she deserved. He was acting out of love. A love that was consistent, abiding and could not let her go into slavery.

Gomer stood, head bowed, expecting a future filled with shame and humiliation. Just when things couldn't look any worse, she heard a voice. She recognized the voice. It seemed to be bidding for her and was willing to pay the regular price to purchase her. As she looked up to see who the speaker was and who was paying the price for her, she saw him. It was her husband, Hosea. The man she despised, deserted and shamed was still willing to buy her back to himself.

When Hosea took her home, she was legally his slave. He could command her to do the things a wife should do for her husband, but he didn't. He took the shackles off of her and told her that she would not call him "Lord or Master." She would call him, "Husband." With one sweeping gesture, all of her rights and privileges as a wife were totally restored. More importantly, the faithful, abiding love of a devoted husband was lavished upon her once again. Hosea's love overlooked his hurt feelings and wounded pride. This love would be Gomer's portion, though she was undeserving and unworthy of it, for the rest of her life.

Hosea's love was meant to be a reflection of God's amazing love for mankind. Gomer brought Hosea nothing but shame, deprivation and sorrow. Yet, he paid the price for her and restored her to the position of being his wife, just as if she had never left. Like Gomer, we turned our backs on the lover of our souls, went our own way and wanted nothing to do with Him. Yet, He sent His son, Jesus, who paid the price on the cross to buy us back again. Then God restores us to Himself again and treats us as if we have never left Him. The story of Hosea and Gomer is a love story, but not in the usual sense. It begins as a one sided love story. Hosea's love for Gomer makes up for her lack of love for him. The same is true of us. God loved us before we ever loved Him and whatever love we have for Him is because He first loved us. I John 4:19.

There are many themes in the prophecy of Hosea. One of the major themes is that the people did not know the Lord. Over and over He stresses this point:

1. There is no knowledge of God in the land- 4:1
2. My people are destroyed for lack of knowledge- 4:6
3. They (the people) have rejected knowledge- 4:6
4. God desires knowledge of Him more than any sacrifice people can make- 6:6

The people's knowledge of their God illustrates Gomer's woeful lack of knowledge of her husband. She didn't think such love was possible. She had totally underestimated his devotion to her. Until we had experienced the love of God, we didn't know He could love us as He does. We thought He was mad at us because of our sins or didn't love us because of our weaknesses and failure. The love story of Hosea and Gomer tells us that God loves us in spite of our shortcomings. His love is pure and everlasting.

Gomer's life of prostitution depicts the sinfulness of man in the lowest, most loathsome form. There were two different kinds of prostitution in Gomer's day. First, there was the common prostitute, the street walker. In today's vernacular, she would be called a "hooker." Then there was the temple prostitute. She was active in the worship of the false god, Baal. Prostitution was prominent in the worshipping of Baal. From the language of the second chapter of Hosea, it seems that Gomer might have been a temple prostitute. This story is written based on that deduction. The women who serve Baal in the temple will be called, "Baal's girls."

Although we cannot tell the exact reason that Gomer left her husband, this story speculates as to why she did. Earlier readings of Hosea's prophecies could lead one to believe that she was just a wanton person returning to her depraved habits. Subsequent readings may lead us to propose different reasons. Perhaps she thought living a life with a prophet was too restricting for her and she found his obedience to Jehovah undesirable. Perhaps the lack of regular income that went with being a prophet was one of the things that drove her back to her former life style.

As Gomer received the love of her husband, which was "above and beyond anything she could ask or think (Ephesians 3:20), let us open our hearts up to God's love. His love is greater than any human love could ever illustrate, and it is free for us all.

The ancient Hebrews had many names for God. One of the primary names used in scripture is that of Jehovah. This name is translated, Lord throughout the Bible. In the love story of Hosea and Gomer the name Jehovah will be widely used along with the more commonly used names of Lord or God.

Although this story concerns people and places in ancient times, a few modern improvisations are used, such as remembering classmates in school or reporting to an office. This is done to make the story palpable to contemporary understanding.

The names of Hosea, Gomer, their children, her father and the prophet Amos are all people who lived and are mentioned in the Bible. This story gives them personality and character. All other names are fictional and are added to tell this important story. Ultimately, it is a story of God's Love. No greater story could ever be told.

CHAPTER ONE

Had he heard God correctly? Did God really mean what he said, or had Hosea imagined these words. It's hard to believe that God would tell him to do such a thing. Marry a harlot? The whole thing seemed so preposterous. Hosea stood staring at the sky for a long time, as if in doing so he could force God to correct Himself or at least give him an explanation. Hosea just stared and stared. No answer was forthcoming, however. The sky remained an unyielding gray. God had said what He had to say and was refusing to say anything further.

Hosea had felt for some time that God was calling him to be a prophet. At certain times he had felt inspired of God to say or do something and the results were always good. His family was pleased to have a prophet in the family and his friends nodded their approval. Now, for the first time Jehovah speaks to him audibly and tells him to do something so bazaar. What would his family and friends think about this? What about his mother? Oh, he could just imagine what she would have to say? It wouldn't be pleasant, that's for sure. Once she gets to harping on the subject, she may never stop.

He considered speaking to his friend, Amos to solicit his opinion. Amos was an established prophet who had come from Judah, the southern kingdom to prophecy in Israel. Yet, Hosea knew that if he was ever going to be a prophet for Jehovah, he had to stand on his own two feet. Nobody else could hear from Jehovah for him, not even another prophet. He had to hear from God on his own.

Hosea decided to rehearse to words that Jehovah had spoken to him, as if in doing so he might discover a loophole to let himself off the hook. God's words were clear, he had not mistaken them. "Go, take to yourself a wife of harlotry…for the people have committed a flagrant harlotry, forsaking the Lord." He couldn't avoid it. He knew what God wanted him to do. He couldn't deny that the people had forsaken the Lord, but what a way to have to proclaim the message.

A number of questions raced through his mind. How do I even find a harlot? This was something that he had never attempted to do before. It is certainly not the kind of a question he could walk up to someone on the street and casually ask. "Excuse me Miss, but might you happen to be a harlot?" How can a prophet of Jehovah walk around town enquiring about how to find a harlot? No easy answers were forthcoming.

"I've got it!" he announced to himself. The answer came so clearly to him, as if a light turned on in his head. The answer was so easy that he wondered why he had not thought of it sooner. Just two blocks from his home stood the Temple of Baal, shining in the bright sunlight. In there were plenty of harlots. Surely, this was the answer. For the first time since he heard the voice of God, he smiled and he began to make plans.

After walking swiftly to the temple, he suddenly halted across the street from the large edifice, glistening in all it's splendor. He had no idea that he would find the large temple so daunting and imposing to him. He stood staring at the door for a long time. Entering it was not as easy as he had imagined. Here was the place where people worshipped the evil god, Baal. Their practices were so corrupt that they were a reproach to his people and were an affront to their God, Jehovah. Here he was, a prophet of God and was planning to go in there.

"Hosea, what are you doing here?" The voice behind him startled him out of his deep thought. He turned to see his friend Amos and was quickly embarrassed by his presence. "You're not thinking of going in there are you?" Amos stared, wonderingly at Hosea "You, whose name means 'savior,' going to worship Baal?"

"Listen, Amos, it is not what it looks like. I've been too embarrassed to tell anyone, but you're a prophet, maybe you will understand. God has spoken to you many times, but he has spoken to me just this once."

"He didn't tell you to worship Baal?"

"No, of course he didn't." Taking a deep breath, Hosea continued, "He told me to marry a harlot…or at least I think he did."

"Why would he tell you to marry a harlot? They cause many people to sin against Jehovah."

"I know, I know." Hosea rejoined. "He said to marry a harlot because 'the people have committed a great harlotry, rebelling against God'."

Amos' eyes brightened and he had a look of someone who just realized something that he previously couldn't figure out. "Now I get it!" Amos responded. "When you spoke I felt the witness of the Spirit of God that what you're saying is true." For a moment neither of them spoke. "And you are wishing that He told you something easy, like calling down fire from Heaven as did Elijah?" he said jokingly.

"My mother might call down fire from somewhere when she hears about this."

Amos couldn't help laughing, "Oh yeah, your mother. Let me guess, you haven't explained this to her yet."

"What do you think?"

"Well, good luck with that one," Amos stated flatly. "Don't worry. She will understand…someday…I think."

"Thanks, a lot. You're such an encouragement," replied Hosea. "Let me ask you this, did you ever wonder how a person would go about finding a harlot?"

"No, I can't say that I have."

"Well, neither have I. Not until this came up. I can't walk up and down the street asking each woman if she is a harlot." Amos smiled, unable to hide his amusement. "It's not funny, Amos. "Anyway, I thought that there are all kinds of harlots in there," he continued, pointing toward the temple. "This way nobody will see me on the street soliciting one of them."

"Okay, that makes sense," answered Amos.

"Boy, I never thought following Jehovah would lead me here," stated Hosea, wistfully.

"Well, I better let you go about your business. Don't worry. Jehovah told you to do this. He'll help and guide you. He always does, you know."

"I know," agreed Hosea. "I'll be seeing you around." As Amos started to make his departure, Hosea added, "pray for me." Amos nodded and waved as he disappeared around the corner.

After staring at the temple for a few more minutes, Hosea, with great trepidation, proceeded to go inside. Inside, the temple was palatial in appearance. Hosea was tempted to admire the beauty of the interior of the edifice. However, he did not think it was appropriate for him, a prophet of Jehovah to do so. It was bad enough just being here. He couldn't help thinking what a pity it was for all this beauty to be for such an evil god as Baal.

"Lord, which one do I choose," he asked God. Again, he got no answer. "You haven't answered me since you first spoke and I'm kind of out on a limb here and could use a little guidance," he pleaded. Then it occurred to him that God told him to marry a harlot. It was up to him to choose which one to marry.

"Can I help you?" Hosea was surprised by the voice behind him. He turned and looked into her eyes and was, immediately at a loss for words. How to begin to explain what he was doing there was a problem that escaped him. While he was deciding what to say first, she repeated the question. "Can I help you? Do you need directions or something?"

"Well, I'm here for a reason," he began.

"Most people are," she responded.

"No, no, you don't understand. I'm not here for the same reason others might be. I…" He was definitely struggling with his conversation. As he looked at this woman, all made up and dressed in her temple clothing, she looked remotely familiar to him. "This is my first time here and, hopefully my only time and, well, it's hard to explain.

She smiled and was obviously amused at his discomfort. She wasn't about to do anything to make it any easier for him. With arms folded, she just smiled and starred at him, waiting for him to make sense. Then he was awakened by recognition.

"Wait a minute. I know you. At least I knew you at one time. You're Gomer, that skinny girl that lived at the end of our street. At least you used to be skinny. Do you remember me? We went to school together. My name is Hosea."

Gomer stared blankly at him. "I'm sorry, I can't place you." She honestly didn't recognize him. "Were we friends or something?"

In his dreams they were more than friends. He had carried the torch of infatuation for her during the entirety of his last year. He wasn't sure if she even knew that he existed. Here he was, face to face with a person that he formerly worshipped from afar, knowing that his admiration was all one sided. After school, he never expected to see her again, especially under such unusual conditions. "No," he replied. "I just knew who you were. I'm not surprised that you don't remember me."

"Well, Mr. Hosea, whom I don't remember, are you going to tell me why you are here, or are you going to just stammer and stutter all day?

. "Just let me get this out. See, I'm a prophet of Jehovah." Her eyes widened and her smile broadened. "You promised not to laugh."

"I'm not laughing," she protested.

"You were about to. Could you kind of stop smiling?" Hosea got the feeling that no matter what he said, she was going to find it amusing and wouldn't hesitate to tell him so.

"I'll try, but you got to admit it. This is kind of funny. A prophet of Jehovah, in Baal's temple, and talking to one of his girls."

"How did you get to be one of Baal's girls, anyway?"

"One question at a time," she ordered. "You never told me why you were here."

"Okay, Okay. Jehovah told me to marry a harlot. I figured the easiest place find a harlot is in here."

"Why did he tell you to marry a harlot? Isn't that kind of strange?"

"He said I was to marry a harlot, because the people have committed a great harlotry by departing from their God."

"Wow! That's incredible! Are you sure you heard Jehovah correctly?"

"If I wasn't absolutely sure, do you think I would be in here, subjecting myself to such ridicule? I was kind of hoping that you might be the girl," he added sheepishly.

"Look, Hosea, you're a nice guy, very naïve, but nice. The thing is, I don't intend to be anyone's wife. Not now, or ever. So you just forget it!" She stalked off without looking back, away from him, around the corner and out of sight.

Hosea however couldn't forget it. He thought about Gomer constantly. When Jehovah told him to marry a harlot, he didn't expect to have such feelings for her. Not this soon, anyway. Daily, he returned to the temple to talk with Gomer. At first she was resistant, but it wasn't long before she was conversing with Hosea in a cordial manner. Soon she seemed to enjoy talking to him. When he brought up the subject of marriage, he was surprised to find her nonresistant. He took great encouragement in this. She even asked questions as to how they might live and what their relationship might be like.

The other temple girls teased her, telling her that she was the only one who ever left the temple to get married. One of Baal's girls marrying one of Jehovah's prophets was just too good. They had to talk about this. Gomer took the teasing in good spirits, even when some called her "Mrs. Jehovah."

Hosea, on the other hand, met with blunt opposition on the part of family and friends. No one teased him. They gave him direct and strong hostility. Nobody was happy for him. "I knew that girl would never amount to anything," they said. "She'll disgrace the whole family. I don't believe God spoke to him, he just wants to marry the tramp. Jehovah would never tell anyone to do such a thing," on and on they went.

The very people that were happy about his call to be a prophet were now opposed to him. The first thing God spoke to him about had turned them against him. It seemed that they resented him for being the very thing that they had saluted him for becoming.

Hosea had expected his mother to be especially obstinate. She didn't fail to fulfill his expectations. No one could belabor a point and carry it out to such lengthy conclusions as Mother. Once she took a stance, it would be easier to move a mountain that to move her. No one that knew her could ever remember her changing her mind on anything. When she opposed something, no one could give an explanation that would make it seem right to her. This was what Hosea was up against. For an entire afternoon she cajoled, she pleaded, she argued against him marrying such a woman of ill repute. She refused to believe that Jehovah had spoken to him. When Hosea finally left for home, his mother still refused to budge from her self-righteous position. She was right and that was all there was to it.

Amidst a whirl of controversy, Hosea and Gomer got married, in a small, quiet ceremony in his back yard. Amos was the best man. Only a few of his relatives showed up. His mother reluctantly attended, making every effort to display her unhappiness. She spoke to Gomer, only in brief, curt statements. A cousin of Gomer's agreed to be the bridesmaid. Her father, Dibliam was in attendance. His quiet demeanor displayed neither pride nor displeasure. Most people seemed anxious to get the whole unhappy affair over with. Finally, the day reached a conclusion.

The first few months of married life were basically happy ones for Gomer and Hosea. Like any other newlyweds, they enjoyed being together, reveling in each other's company. They walked, hand in hand down the streets, through the parks and market places. Anyone could see that they were deeply in love.

Hosea was so happy that he almost forgot about the command of Jehovah that their marriage was to demonstrate to the people their infidelity towards God. He wondered how his happiness could ever reveal this. He never spoke about it to Gomer and he secretly hoped that Jehovah would change his mind and allow their happiness to go on forever. Maybe God would reward him for his obedience and that was all that was required. After all, when God told Abraham to offer his son, Isaac as a sacrifice, he was not required to go through with it. Maybe God would do the same for him.

Gomer also remained silent about her past life. She didn't seem to miss it at all. Like Hosea, she lived in the present, making every effort to forget the past altogether. They began to make plans, dreaming of a happy future. Little did they know that their Heaven of happiness would one day come to an abrupt end, and on that day, everything that seemed so good would start to go wrong and no power on earth could stop it.

CHAPTER TWO

"Hosea, quick, call the doctor! I think it's time!" Gomer was screaming at him as she held her stomach in pain. Seized with panic, Hosea started quickly for the door. Then he abruptly stopped in his tracks. "Why are you stopping?" she demanded. "I need the doctor, now."

"The doctor started his country rounds yesterday," Hosea replied, nervously. "He won't be back for days."

"Then get Heather, the mid-wife, but do it quickly." For a moment, Hosea couldn't seem to get his feet to move and was frozen where he stood. "What's the matter with you?" Gomer screeched. "Don't just stand there. I need Heather. Go get her."

"Heather, yes Heather. I can get her," he babbled. In his panic he, momentarily forgot where Heather lived but wildly ran for the door, hoping to remember as he sped along. It didn't work. He reached the door and had no idea where Heather lived. He had no choice but to ask Gomer. Momentarily she seemed at ease so he asked, "Where does Hannah live?"

"You know, up on the hill by the orchard."

"Of course, I knew that. What's the matter with me?"

"Calm down husband," Gomer serenely stated. She seemed to be enjoying a brief moment of tranquility. "Women have been having babies for centuries. I'll be okay." Then another pain pierced her abdomen. "But hurry," she shouted.

"Calm down, but hurry. Okay! Okay, here I go," having said that, he disappeared out the door. He arrived at Heather's house and frantically began pounding on the door. Heather seemed reluctant as she opened the door. "Heather hurry, my wife needs you. She is going into labor." Heather's response was puzzling to Hosea, as well as frustrating. She merely nodded her head and slowly began gathering her things. "Come on, Heather, hurry up, Gomer is in labor. What's the matter with you?"

"I'm coming, Hosea," she slowly answered. " It is my duty, after all."

"Your duty? What do you mean? Don't you want to help us?" He couldn't understand her attitude at all.

"We've got nothing against you, Hosea. We all think the world of you. It's just…"

"Just what, my wife? You don't like my wife?"

"It's nothing personal, we hardly know her."

"'We.' Why do you say 'we?' Have you been discussing this with anyone?' Heather remained silent. That's when it hit him. Hosea and Gomer had been so wrapped up in their happiness that neither of them had even considered what other people might think about their marriage. They didn't hear the quiet whispers or notice the heads shaking. The sudden perception of the public opinion about his union with Gomer overwhelmed him.

"Like I say, Hosea," she continued, "we all love you. We just think you could have done better. She was one of Baal's girls. We all know what they do."

"But, she's changed. She left all of that behind. Can't you see that?"
"Are you sure? Do people ever really change? Can a fish fly? Can a bird swim? Oh, I don't want to hurt you for anything in the world, but somebody's got to tell you." Hosea remained silent even though he was boiling mad. "I'm coming to help her, but I wouldn't be the least bit surprised if she wound up right back where you found her."

They walked in silence back to Hosea's house. He was afraid to speak for fear that what he said would be a poor representative of a prophet of Jehovah. He sat in the living room, waiting for the birth of his first child. His thoughts were consumed with Heather's unkind words. "So this is what people thought of his wife? Well, if they didn't like her they could just stay away from him," he petulantly imagined. As his emotions fluctuated between anger and self- pity, he heard the voice of Jehovah. This was the second time that he heard the voice of God and he was astonished at his own emotion. He wasn't in the mood to hear the voice of God. It annoyed him. He wished Jehovah would speak when he felt a little more spiritual, but, there was no mistaking it. Jehovah was speaking to him and he knew that he must listen.

God told him that he was going to have a son and that he was to call his name "Jezreel." Hosea wanted to ask God why, but before he would even voice the question, God gave the explanation. Jezreel was the place where King Jehu had usurped the throne in a bloody insurrection. Hosea's son's name meant that Jehovah was about to bring his kingdom to an end.

Heather appeared silently in the doorway. Then Hosea detected the cry of the baby. "My son," he said, "how is he?" Heather looked surprised, but didn't even ask how he knew that the baby was a boy. He didn't ask about Gomer, lest she give some more of her free advice about things that were none of her business. In silence she gathered her things and left for home.

Hosea quickly entered the bedroom. His senses were still tingling from having heard to voice of Jehovah. He was greeted by his wife who was broadly smiling for another reason, the birth of their son. "Here, Daddy, meet your new son." She was obviously overjoyed. "Isn't he handsome? Shall we call him Beeri, after your father or Diblaim, after mine?" She was so excited that he dreaded telling her what Jehovah had said.

"Neither one, Honey, we can't name him after either one of our fathers. Her smile quickly faded as her eyes looked questioningly at him. Hosea hated to see her enthusiasm curbed. He wanted her happiness to continue as long as possible.

"What do you mean, we can't? We can name him whatever we want." She instinctively hugged the baby closer to her chest.

"Jehovah has spoken to me again." He proceeded to tell her about the voice and the message it contained. The longer he spoke, the deeper her frown seemed to grow. He hated to disappoint her. He loved it when she smiled and they were in complete agreement. Yet, he knew that he had to be obedient to Jehovah.

"But tradition is very important in my family. Doesn't Jehovah understand that?" She couldn't keep the sarcasm out of her voice.

"Please, Gomer, don't say that. When Jehovah speaks, I have to…we have to obey him. Surely you know that."

"Maybe you do, but I don't," she protested. "Baal would never have made such a demand." This was the first time in their marriage that the name of this pagan deity was mentioned. Hosea looked stricken, as if someone hat hit him with his fist. Immediately, Gomer was sorry that she had spoken in such a manner. As disappointed as she was, Gomer found herself agreeing with her husband and allowing Jehovah name their first son. However, she made Hosea promise that the next child would be named after someone in one of their families. Hosea knew that he really couldn't make this promise, but, in hopes of making peace between him and his wife, he did so anyway.

The next child was a girl. Again Heather assisted in the delivery. This time she kept her opinions to herself and Hosea said as little as possible. Before the delivery, Gomer reminded Hosea of his promise in regards to naming the child. He reminded her, that if Jehovah should speak again, they must obey. They both hoped that Jehovah would not speak. They both hoped in vain. For the third time in his life, Hosea heard the voice of God. As thrilled as he was about hearing God's voice, Hosea was equally as apprehensive about breaking the news to Gomer.

God told Hosea to name his daughter, Lo-ruhamah meaning "not pitied or no mercy." The message was clear, that the people of Israel were living in such an ungodly way that they did not deserve His mercy. Again an argument broke out. This time it did not last as long as before and Gomer never mentioned the name of Baal. Again she submitted to God and her husband. In her heart, though, it was another matter. Inwardly she began to wish that she and Hosea was not serving Jehovah, but was serving Baal.

Finally the day came for the birth of their second son. This time the doctor delivered and this symbolized to Gomer that things were going to be different. She intended to have more to say in naming this child.

Hosea was not surprised to hear the voice of God telling him what to name the child. His name was to be Lo-ammi, meaning, " not my people." The message that this name was intended to deliver was that God's people had so rebelled against Him that God no longer considered them His people.

When Hosea entered the bedroom and deliver the message to his wife she exploded with pent-up anger. "What is it with this God of yours? Is he so domineering that he can't let us name even one of our own children? How can he be so cruel?" Gomer was so angry that she was trembling. Not knowing what to say, Hosea remained silent. He hoped that her anger would subside. It did not. Then with a voice that was deliberate and calculated, she spoke words that drove a proverbial dagger through Hosea's heart. "I wish that we were both serving Baal," she said.

'You don't mean that. Please tell me that you don't," he desperately pleaded.

"I do mean it," she shouted with tears streaming down her cheeks. "Serving Jehovah is too restricting, too demanding. He's a cruel taskmaster and I hate Him."

"I didn't know that Jehovah was going to name our children, but I'm His prophet. I must obey, what else can I do?"

"But you don't know what it is like to serve and worship Baal. I do. I've been on both sides of the fence and worshipped in both religions. To me, Baal worship is better."

"With it's carnal practices and promiscuity? How can you say that it's better?"

"But don't you see? That's the point. You can live any way you want to. To serve Jehovah you have to keep His law and obey His voice. Baal worship frees us from all of that."

Hosea was shocked that anyone knowing the ways of Baal and the ways of Jehovah would say that Baal treated his people better. Anytime that he argued with anyone in the past, he challenged the other person to compare the two religions with confidence that they would find Jehovah worshipper better than Baal worship. Here he was debating with his wife, who had compared the two religions and found Baal better. What could he say? The basis of his whole argument was gone.

"Listen, Hosea, what does Jehovah promise to His worshippers?"

"You know, if we hearken to His voice that He would bless us in every way. Well, like it says in our Law. If we listen to God and do what He says we will be blessed in our families, our cattle, our crops and in every way."

"That's exactly what Baal promises only you don't have to be so perfect to get those blessings. You don't have to be holy. You can have as many love partners as you want. Baal loves you enough to bless you, no matter what you do."

"That can't be true."

"It is," she insisted. "If a couple is having difficulty conceiving a child, all he has to do is sleep with one of Baal's girls and their infidelity is cured. If a man has a piece of ground that doesn't seem to produce anything, if he takes one of Baal's girls out there, the land will start growing things. See how much better it is? No holiness! No faithfulness to one mate. No domineering God."

"Those things that you speak of, they're an abomination. No one can be blessed for doing such things."

"Not when you serve a God that demands perfection the way Jehovah does. He is a jealous, spiteful God. Baal, on the other hand offers personal freedom and individual expression. With him, we don't have to be all alike and believe the same thing. Baal doesn't have all these demands and commandments. He is not trying to make puppets out of us the way Jehovah does."

"It's God's commandments that keep our people true and consistent," he answered in a voice that was almost a plea for her to see his point.

"No, it's those commandments that keep people enslaved. Thou shalt not this and thou shalt not that. And whatever you do, don't walk ten feet on the Sabbath Day, she added sarcastically. She knew that she was exaggerating, but, now that she was making her point, she wasn't about to lose momentum. "Is Jehovah afraid that He will get tired out trying to keep up with you?"

"Baal's laws may look like freedom but, in the end they will enslave you. You watch and see if they don't." With those words, Hosea turned and left the house. He could see that there was no point in trying to reason with Gomer now. Hopefully, she would calm down later on and continue to follow Jehovah. Hosea was to learn that this hope was in vain.

Something different happened that day. Something dark and sinister had come between Hosea and his wife. Once it was there, there seemed to be no removing of it. At times they would both try to be cordial to one another, but their relationship was never to be the same again. Baal had crowded his way into their home and with him came a disturbing shadow that could not be dislodged.

Hosea still believed that Baal's promise of freedom would only lead to slavery. Gomer did not believe it, but in later years she would learn in bitter reality just how right her husband was.

CHAPTER THREE

So their argument continued, off and on for the next five years. They didn't argue every day, but this unresolved issue clouded the rest of their marriage. Gone were the happy days of when they were first married. Hosea wished that he could recover them, somehow. Perhaps Gomer did, too, but they now seemed like a long lost time. Hosea often ached to hold his wife, knowing that she would find contentment in his arms. He wished that he could reach out and take her hand and having her respond the way she used to. There was a time when her positive responses came automatic. Now, he was never sure if she wanted him to touch her or not.

It's hard to believe that so much time could elapse with them in this midnight of uncertainty. Day followed day, the children were growing up but their grasp of the essence of being husband and wife seemed to be slipping away. Although he was not sure of her feelings, Hosea still loved her as much as ever and wished he could get her back as she was before.

It seemed that the only way to resolve this dilemma was for him to turn his back on Jehovah and become a Baal worshipper. This he could never do. Yet she refused to honor Jehovah, insisting that Baal worship was better. In her mind, Jehovah was the one who was tearing them apart. When he pointed out that Jehovah was the reason that they were together in the first place, she scoffed. He wondered if she still loved him or even if she ever had. He ached to hold her, to kiss her and to love her. Didn't she feel any of that?

Sometime in the second year of this limbo living, she started doing something that eventually became a habitual pattern. She began leaving the house and being gone all day. At first, when questioned where she had been, she would be evasive. Later, she would say that she was visiting friends. Hosea knew that it was unlikely that she had any friends outside the temple. He didn't voice this opinion for the sake of saving an argument. Was she doing what she did before? Was she being a temple girl in the day time and coming home to barely speak to him at night? Hosea tortured himself with questions. Then one day, he decided to ask her.

"Where have you been," he asked as she walked in the door. He was making every effort to act casual.

"Out visiting friends." She sternly replied. "Is that a crime?"

For the first time he decided to question her answer. "I didn't know that you had so many friends."

"I have enough and I visit them often."

"Who? Who are your friends?" he pressed her.

With this question, she exploded in rage. "Why do you ask? Are you checking up on me? Don't I have any rights, any freedom? You're as bad as that Jehovah that you worship." She tried to say something as mean as possible so he would stop questioning her. It worked for a while, until the day he decided to question her again.

A long time later, he again questioned her as to her whereabouts and again she responded by making her actions seem as normal as possible. He decided to tell her that Heather told him that she had seen her going to the temple. This was a bad mistake.

"Oh she would say something like that. She never liked me, none of your friends did. Those worshippers of Jehovah did nothing but stick their noses up at me. They ought to have their tongues cut out for being such busy bodies." Having said that, she grabbed her shawl and headed for the door.

"Gomer, where are you going," he asked. He was sorry that he had brought up the subject of her temple visits.

"Out," she shouted as loud as she could. And you better not have your nosey friends follow me this time." Out she went, slamming the door so hard that it made little Lo-Ammi cry. This time she was gone for a week. When she finally returned, neither one of them said anything to each other. Days of silence went by. The picture was coming clear to Hosea, he was losing her. She was like a large rock rolling down hill and he was powerless to stop her.

Hosea was so wrapped up in his problem that he didn't even think of the things that Jehovah had told him about his marriage in the first place. He couldn't see what was happening as part of God's plan. He had forgotten all of this in his desperate attempt to keep his wife from leaving. He wished that he could find the right words to say that would persuade her to stay and be his wife. He could not. Words had failed him, in fact, they had made things worse.

Then the day came that Gomer broke her silence but it was not good news, it was the worst. Everything that Hosea had feared was now happening before his very eyes. "I'm leaving," she announced, "and this time it's for good."

"No, please don't," he pleaded, "I need you, the kids need you. Don't go."

"I have to. I can't live here like this. It would be living a lie. I worship Baal, not Jehovah and you…you're just the opposite."

"Can't we just try one more time? We can work things out. I know we can."

"How?" she questioned. "How can we work things out? Are you going to worship Baal?" He didn't know what to say. "Can we compromise? Can we worship one god for half a year and the other one for the second half? You're Jehovah would not go along with that."

"Gomer, please…don't go." At this point he would have begged if he thought it would help, but he knew that it would not. Even if it would change things, he didn't know what more he could say.

"I have to," she curtly responded and then she was out the door leaving her husband, the prophet in tears.

A month or so later Gomer returned home to get some of her things. When Hosea saw her walking up the road he gathered the two youngest children together and told them, "Rahumah, Ammi, plead with your mother and ask her to come home and be my wife again."

"Isn't she still your wife?" Rahumah asked.

"She is not living like my wife nor is she living like your mother. Will you ask her?"

"Yes Daddy," they both replied in unison.

After Gomer came in and then entered the bedroom, the two little ones followed her in. "Mommy," Rahumah said. No answer. Gomer was considering what to take with her and what she no longer needed. "Mommy," Rahumah repeated. This time she turned around.

"What is it, honey?"

"Are you going to come home and be our Mommy again?" As Gomer looked down into the sad, tearful eyes, her heart nearly broke and her resolve, right along with it.

"I can't, Sweetie. I can't live here like this and I can't take you with me. Your Dad will take good care of you. "The two children had no idea what she was talking about, but they knew that she was telling them that she couldn't stay. After a long silence she asked them, "Where is your big brother? Where is Jezreel?"

"He stays in his room most of the time since you went away," replied Rahumah. "He says it is Daddy's fault that you left home." Gomer didn't know what to say. She too had certainly blamed Hosea.

"He says he is going to be a p'iest of Ball," added Ammi.

"A priest of Baal," corrected Gomer. "When he grows up, he can be. It will be his choice."

"Please Mommy, won't you come home," begged little Rahumah, who continued to cry, bitterly.

Even though Gomer's heart ached for her children, she answered, "I can't. I can't live the way your father lives, but I know that he will take good care of you."

The children continued to cry as they silently pleaded with their mother. Those innocent faces covered with tears became too much for Gomer. Quickly she stood and started for the door. . She stopped before she got there, turned and said, "Always remember, no matter what, Mommy loves you both." Then she went out the door. Once again she was gone. Rahumah and Ammi stood in muted silence. They both sat down on the bed and cried uncontrollably. Their little minds knew that she wasn't coming back. Before they had hoped that she would, but now they knew the truth. Their hope had gone out the door with their mother.

A few minutes later, their father had come into the bedroom. Both of the children flew into his arms. "We couldn't do it, Daddy. We couldn't get her to come home. She just wouldn't stay."

"I know," said Hosea.

"We tried," Ammi continued.

"I know that you did. And I thank you for that." After a pause he added, "Maybe I was wrong to ask you to do it."

Later that day, as they sat at the dinner table picking at their food, Rahumah asked her father a question, Daddy, why did you change our names?"

"I don't know what you mean, honey."

"We've always been Lo-Rahumah and Lo-Ammi, but when you asked us to speak to Mommy you called us Rahumah and Ammi."

"Well, you see, when you were born, Jehovah told me to name you Lo-Rahumah because the name means 'not pitied or no mercy.' This is because all the people are living so wickedly that they do not deserve God's mercy."

"Jehovah named us?"

"That's right."

"That is so cool. Isn't that cool, Ammi?" The little boy nodded in agreement. "So what does Ammi's name mean?"

"Well you see, Lo-Ammi means, 'Not my people.' The people are living in such a way that they do not deserve to be called God's People."

"But that still doesn't explain why you stopped calling us 'Lo' before our names."

"Yeah, 'splain' it, Daddy," contributed little Ammi.

"You see, 'Lo' means 'no or not,'" continued Hosea. "It indicates that God's people are not worthy of his mercy or even to be called His people. God's people have made Him real sad."

"As sad as we are for Mommy leaving," asked Rahumah.

"Sadder," replied Hosea.

"God must be real sad," said Ammi.

"He is. But do you know what," continued Hosea. "God loves His people so much that, even though they do not deserve his mercy he gives it to them anyway. And even though God's people leave Him, if they come back, He would take them back in a moment."

"Even though they left Him, God would take them back, just like that," asked a bewildered Rahumah.

"Just like that!" answered Hosea, snapping his fingers.

Like you would take Mommy back, right Daddy," she asked.

"Just like that!" he repeated, again snapping his fingers. "You see, God's mercy is new every morning, and it lasts forever. "We never get so bad or wander so far from God that He wouldn't forgive us and take us back any time we return to Him. So, in honor of God's love and mercy, I'm going to keep calling you Rahumah and Ammi. How does that sound to you?"

"Great," replied Rahumah. "Right, Ammi?"

"Right," he answered with a big grin.

Even though the children were happy with their new names they were still sad over their mother leaving. Those were the saddest of days. A dark cloud darkened their days and tears were their portion every night. Even though they were determined not to do so, every night they cried and cried until they cried themselves to sleep.

CHAPTER FOUR

"Daddy, you're burning my pancake!" screamed Ammi. His is expression revealed the panic he was feeling. Suddenly pulled from his transfixion, Hosea looked down at the griddle. Sure enough the pancake was burning and smoke began to fill the kitchen. Drifting into deep thought patterns was typical of his behavior since Gomer had left two months ago. He tried and tried to stay focused in the present, but he couldn't seem to help himself. Many times he found himself emerging from involuntary day-dreams.

"Why had she left? What could he have done to stop her? Maybe if I had done this or maybe if I had done that it would have made a difference. Over and over he kept torturing himself with self-accusations and questions.

He knew that Jehovah had told him that his marriage was to be an object lesson to the people, but he didn't know that living this lesson was going to hurt so much. He didn't feel like he could stand it. Did Israel's sin bring this much pain to the heart of God? He didn't just love Gomer because God told him to, he loved her sincerely. He couldn't imagine life without her. His heart was breaking and he knew that Jehovah's was too. Here he was, a prophet with a broken heart serving a God who also had a broken heart.

Hosea looked down at the pancake he was trying to cook and it was useless. It was overcooked on one side and raw on the other. He was attempting to cook pancakes for Rahumah and Ammi but he was failing miserably. He couldn't seem to do much of anything these days. Every time he tried to do something constructive, he found himself drifting off into the oasis of his dream world.

Yet, during these times of pain and confusion, Jehovah seemed to be very close to him and spoke to him often. Usually, Jehovah's statements were about something he was experiencing or seeing. Inevitably, there would be a comparison of Hosea's experience to the condition of the people. Even now as he dumped the useless, partially cooked pancake into the garbage can he heard Jehovah say, "My people are like a cake not turned." Hosea immediately understood the meaning. The people were half serving God and half serving Baal. They were, therefore, committed to neither. Trying to serve both God and Baal had left them in a half- hearted state of existence, like a pancake that was burnt on one side and raw on the other.

The remainder of breakfast continued without any problems. The children enjoyed their pancakes and forgot about the burnt one. As the children were leaving the table, footsteps were heard at the door. It was Hosea's mother, making her weekly visit since Gomer had left. The children were excited, yelling "Grandma!" and rushing into her waiting arms. Hosea groaned. She had visited regularly since her son had lost his wife. Every time she came, she became "Mrs. I-told-you-so."

"Mother, please, I don't want to argue," he said.

"I didn't come to argue," she insisted. "I came to see to it that the children were fed properly."

"We had pancakes," shouted an excited Ammi.

"It smells like you had burnt pancakes. Do you burn all of their food, Hosea? I shudder to think about what you and the kids are eating."

"It was one pancake, Mother, just one. We're eating just fine." This was the way it was every time Mother came to visit. The children were too young to comprehend her sarcasm, so they always welcomed her with enthusiasm. Hosea dreaded every visit and was always happy to see her go. Before their marriage, his mother made no effort to conceal her opposition. After Gomer was gone, she constantly reminded Hosea that she knew his marriage would fail and that he could have done better. Hosea felt bad enough about the circumstances but Mother ranted on relentlessly. She was convinced that he had shamed the whole family.

As always Hosea kissed her goodbye when she was leaving and as always he sighed with relief after she left. Many others came to visit during those days. They all shared his mother's opinion. Hosea wondered if his mother had sent them. He reminded each one that their visit wasn't necessary, but they all insisted that they came by to cheer him up. Yet they never failed to get "their two cents in" about how they knew that his marriage would not last. Hosea wanted to say, like Job, "Miserable comforters are you all," but he wasn't as heartless as they were. Therefore, he always politely thanked them for their visit.

The only visitor who understood how Hosea was feeling was Amos. He had been privy to God's commandment to Hosea about his marriage. Amos always encouraged Hosea to continue to put his faith in Jehovah. He kept reminding him that God could turn his mourning into joy and that in the end he would be glad he did what Jehovah told him to. Hosea always felt encouraged by Amos' visits.

After Mother finally left, Hosea decided to take a walk, to clear his head. Remembering the burnt pancake, he knew that he had to get a grip on his emotions. He had not walked far before he again drifted into his mental prison of torture. Again he tormented himself with the same answerless questions. They were the same questions as before. Why had she left? What should he have done? Again there were no answers, just more heartache.

As he walked, he felt something tickling his cheek. Touching his cheek, he felt wetness. It was tears on his face. He had been crying and didn't even know it. This was typical of his emotions these days. Some times when he was out walking he felt guilty for leaving the house. He ought to be home for her. He knew that this was irrational because she wasn't there.

Suddenly, he felt a sense of anger. This was not anger at Gomer for leaving, but anger at Jehovah. This was really His fault. Were it not for His command to Hosea to marry a harlot, all of this heart ache would not exist. Certainly Hosea would not have taken it upon himself to marry one of Baal's girls. He knew that his marriage was intended to be an object lesson to Israel for rebelling against Jehovah, but why did he have to be the example? What was the matter with the high priest? Why couldn't he bear this burden, was he too busy? On and on these rhetorical questions went. He knew it was pointless to vent his anger at Jehovah, but he decided to indulge himself anyway.

Just as Hosea was about to plunge in the depths of self-pity, a dove flew overhead. It was so close and flew so erratic that he thought for a moment it might hit him. He began to watch the bird. It seemed to be going nowhere in particular. It just flittered in one direction and then another. "You're acting like a crazy bird," he said. "You don't seem to know what you're doing? What, did your mate leave you too?"

Just then, even in the midst of his self-pity and anger, Jehovah spoke again. "My people are like a silly dove, without heart." That's all He said. Hosea was beginning to recognize God's voice so much better than he did that first day. It was a voice that he was hearing more and more often. It was the only thing that seemed to lift his spirits as it did, once again at this moment.

The message was clear. It was one that Hosea would be responsible to proclaim to the people. Like this silly bird, Israel had flitted from one political alliance to another and from one god to another. Even as Gomer had committed herself to no particular lover, the people had committed themselves to no particular god. Their indecisiveness had left them with no solid purpose, just like this silly dove.

Jehovah's message had appeased Hosea's anger, even though part of him did not want to let it go. He partly wanted to be mad, yet despite himself, he could not. Jehovah's voice worked like a balm, soothing his wounded spirit. It always had that effect. With a clearer head and a lighter spirit, he headed for home.

A few days later, Hosea was surprised by a visit from Dibliam, Gomer's father. He knew that her father would be as disappointed as he was about Gomer's behavior. Just when it looked like she had turned her life around, she went back to her past.

"Dad, come on in," said Hosea, greeting him at the door.

"It is good to see you, Hosea," Dibliam said after seating himself at the table. "Have you heard anything from Gomer?"

"No. Not since she left. Have you?"

"No," replied the elderly gentleman. "I was so disappointed when she left you and the kids." After a long pause he continued, "And then to go back to being one of Baal's girls...well, it just broke my heart."

"Mine too," deadpanned Hosea. At this point, both of the men were close to tears. Then the two youngest children came in the back door.

"Grandpa!" they cried as they came running and threw themselves in their grandfather's arms. Even though they were both very excited to see him, Dibliam could see the evident disappointment in their eyes. These were two sad children. He wondered if Gomer could see their expressions, would it make a difference to her. They were too young to be so brokenhearted. He wished he could say something to make it better for them, but he couldn't. Nobody could.

As Rahumah and Ammi drew up chairs to sit on each side of him, Dibliam asked, "Where is Jezreel?"

"He stays in his room most of the time. I guess he reads a lot. He doesn't join in family activities much." Hosea paused as his father-in-law looked askance at Hosea, not understanding what he was being told. Therefore, Hosea continued, "You see, he blames me for his mother leaving. He seems to see her side of the situation. He claims that he wants to be a priest of Baal when he grows up. I'm not sure if just says that to hurt me or if he really means it."

"He means it," interjected Rahumah. "He talks about it all the time."

"Do you think it would help if I talked to him?" asked Dibliam.

"No, I don't think it would," answered Hosea. "I wish that it would, but it might just make matters worse."

Continuing to drape one arm around each of his grandchildren, Dibliam said to Hosea, "I was planning on visiting Gomer in the temple. I was wondering if there was anything that you would like to tell her...or perhaps to send to her?"

"No I guess not."

"Daddy sends her stuff all the time," said Rahumah.

"Rahumah, please, let me tell him," he chided his daughter. "I don't want a lot of people to know this. I don't even want her to know this, but I am supporting Gomer. She thinks that her support is coming from the Baal Temple treasuries, but it isn't, it is coming from me."

"But why…why are you doing this? She all but stopped being your wife."

"She may have stopped being my wife but I will never stop being her husband. I don't want any false god or his priests taking credit for her support. As long as I am alive I will support your daughter. No matter what she has done, I love her and I always will. Baal will not be credited for supporting the wife of a prophet of Jehovah."

"But how do you do this," asked Dibliam.

"Temple outsiders can designate gifts for individuals inside. She probably things these food stuffs are coming from one of her clients. She must never know and so I'm asking you to promise to never tell her"

Dibliam sighed and took a few moments he replied. "Why don't you want her to know, Hosea?"

"I guess it's my attempt to still make some sort of a claim on her. I love your daughter, sir. When Jehovah commanded me to marry a harlot and I chose Gomer, He gave me such an overwhelming love for her. Everybody thinks that I'm a fool. Well, I don't care what they think. I love her and I'm going to be whatever kind of a husband I can be to her. So please promise me that you will not tell her about my support of her."

"I understand. I promise," avowed Dibliam. "It pains me to see you so heartbroken, but I'm proud that you love her. I couldn't ask for a better son-in-law."

Soon Dibliam bid his farewells to Hosea and the children. The older gentleman arose and made his way out the door and down the street. With both children silently leaning on him, Hosea watched Dibliam slowly walk down the street, around the corner and out of sight.

"He is sad, isn't he, Daddy?" Rahumah asked.

"Yes he is."

"Just like us," added Ammi.

"That's right," answered Hosea, "just like us."

"And just like Jehovah," continued Rahumah. Hosea didn't say anything. He didn't have to. He was amazed at his children's grasp of the whole heart breaking situation.

After his father-in-law left and the children had gone out to play, Hosea was alone in the house. Suddenly the silence of the house seemed to overwhelm him like a child caught under a large blanket and couldn't get his head out. Immediately, he had trouble breathing in the midst of this oppressive, smothering silence. Tears came to his eyes as he began to believe that this overpowering quietness was be with him for the rest of his life.

CHAPTER FIVE

"Gomer's back!" shouted Sarah to a gaggle of Baal's girls who were clustered and engrossed in conversation.

"She's back here?" asked an astounded Hannah. "What on earth for?"

"After she was married and had a family, she comes back here?" contributed Bianca. "Some people don't know when they are well off."

"Well, I for one will be happy to see her. I've missed Gomer," remarked Rachel. "In fact, I think I will go and welcome her back." She started for the apartment assigned to Gomer. Sarah and Hannah began to quietly follow along behind.

"I think I'll pass on that," stated Bianca. "I'm afraid I can't muster up any enthusiasm about her decision to return here. If I go with you girls, she'll read my thoughts for sure."

"Are you jealous, because she got married and you never did?" asked Hannah.

"No, I don't think I'm jealous," responded Bianca. "But I know one thing. If I were married to a good man and had a few kids by him, you wouldn't catch me back here."

"Even to a prophet of Jehovah?" asked Sarah.

"I wouldn't care if he was a prophet of Zeus. If he loved me and provided for me, I'd stick with him."

"Well, I think she is foolish, too," replied Hannah. "But she was my friend and I plan on continuing to be her friend. I don't know why she left her husband. She may have had a very good reason."

"Me too," continued Rachel. "I'll support Gomer no matter what she decides to do. That's what friends do, they always support one another."

"Well, count me out," countered Bianca.

"Wait a minute," said Sarah, "I think I understand what's going on with you. You knew her husband, didn't you?" After a pause, she added, "and, If I remember correctly, you used to like him."

This newly revealed piece of information got Rachel all excited. "Is that true? You used to like Gomer's husband? What's his name anyway?"

"Hosea," answered a tight lipped Bianca.

Sarah couldn't resist needling Bianca and milking every bit of juice that she could out of her victim's discomfort. "Tell me, Bianca, does mentioning Hosea's name get the old heart pumping faster. Is the flame of love starting to fire up, is it?"

"Then you are jealous," declared Rachel. "Not just because she got married but because she married your old flame."

"Come on," answered Bianca. "He was never my boyfriend or anything. I just kind of liked him, but that was a long time ago."

"You know what they say," replied Rachel. "Let's see, how does it go? Oh I remember they say that 'the first flame never quite burns out.' Isn't that it?"

"Who says that?" Bianca wanted to know. "You just made that up, Rachel."

"I did not. I heard somebody say it…sometime. I think it was my uncle."

"Your uncle doesn't count. It's got to be somebody famous that said it for it to be a saying."

"But, what about it," asked an impartial Sarah, "has the old flame burned out? I mean…it doesn't matter if it is a saying or not, what matters is, is it true? Bianca, do you still have feelings for Hosea after all these years?"

After a long pause during which Bianca endured six enquiring eyes staring at her, she finally answered. "Alright, alright, I'll admit it. I always did like Hosea. But it doesn't make any difference. I don't think he even knew I was alive because he had eyes only for Gomer." The girls continued to walk with no one talking. They all seemed to sense that Bianca wasn't finished with her confession. "It's kind of pathetic, I guess," she finally continued. "I used to stare at him while he was staring at her."

Sarah affectionately took Bianca by the arm. "It's not pathetic to like someone, Bianca. We've all been through it. Love is never easy."

"Yeah," continued Hannah, "I can sure vouch for that. Do you girls remember Andrew who lived across town by the fish market?"

"The one with red hair and freckles," enquired Rachel.

"The very same," answered Hannah. "Well, I used to follow him around, all through town."

"Did he ever notice you?" asked Bianca.

"He sure did. He used to turn around and insult me all the time, while his friends laughed. He called me his ugly hound dog, but that didn't stop me. I had it so bad that I followed him no matter what he called me."

"Did you ever get over him?" asked Sarah.

"Yeah, about five years after he married that Rebecca girl who lived next door to him."

"Rebecca, that ugly little skinny thing?" asked Sarah "You mean that he preferred her to you? That doesn't say much for his intelligence."

"Yeah," continued Rachel, "and you are anything but ugly."

"Well, I don't think I look much like a hound dog either," remarked Hannah. All the girls had a good laugh about Hannah's assessment of her appearance as they continued toward Gomer's place.

Bianca wanted to return to the subject to reaffirm her point. "However, I would still think Gomer was being foolish, even If I didn't know and like her husband."

"Well, I guess everyone is entitled to their own opinion, but in the long run, it is what Gomer decides for herself that matters," replied Rachel. "Don't you think so, Bianca?"

"I suppose so," answered Bianca. "Besides, I guess if Hannah was Andrew's hound dog, I could be Hosea's hound dog."

"Every one of us is somebody's hound dog, at one time or another," added a smiling Sarah.

They were in this light hearted attitude as they arrived at Gomer's front door. They all stood and looked at one another for a few seconds. "Well," offered Rachel, "I guess we should just knock on the door and see if she is home."

"Wait," said Bianca, "please don't say anything about what I told you about liking Hosea or how I feel about her coming back."

"Of course not," answered Sarah. "Oh I might mention something about you being Hosea's hound dog, but that's about it." All the girls laughed at this. They were still laughing when Gomer opened the door without anyone knocking.

"I was wondering who was talking and laughing outside my door. We're you ever going to knock to come in?" asked Gomer. "What's so funny anyway?"

"Oh, nothing," answered Hannah.

"That's a lot of laughing for nothing," answered Gomer.

"Well, it doesn't seem so funny anymore," answered Sarah. "You sort of had to be there, right, girls?" They all answered in the affirmative. Gomer didn't care what they had been laughing at. She was so glad to see them. Each one embraced her as they enter her home. All five of them were delighted to be together again. After they were seated, everyone seemed to be unsure how to open the conversation.

Finally Bianca began. "We were all surprised that you moved back here for good and returned to the temple."

"Yeah," continued Hannah, "we were always glad for you to visit, but we didn't thing you would come pack permanently. I mean…we heard you talk about it, but didn't think you would actually do it."

"But, were glad to see you, anyway," stated Sarah. She was attempting to sound more inviting that the other two had sounded.

"I just couldn't stay there and live like that," remarked Gomer. "It all got to be just too much."

"What got to be too much?" asked Bianca." How could living with a husband and three kids be too much?" Bianca had sounded more sarcastic than she had intended to. This earned her a reproving stare from Rachel.

"You don't know what it was like," countered Gomer. "None of you know what it was like. Those worshippers of Jehovah have too many restricting rules. You try living like that and see how long you last." Everyone was stunned into silence. Gomer had matched Bianca's sarcasm and then some. She used to be the picture of patience but not anymore. Gomer had flown into this rage so quickly and so easily. "That's right, before you go judging me, you try living like that. Then come and talk to me."

"We didn't come here to judge you, Gomer," replied Rachel.

"No we didn't," added Sarah. "We just wanted to welcome you back." She looked at Bianca and Rachel, imploring them to support her statement. Being surprised by Gomer's response, they both answered in the affirmative.

"Gomer?" asked Rachel, "you said we didn't know what it was like living like you did. What was it like? Tell us."

"You've got to eat one thing and you can't eat another," replied Gomer. "You can't do anything on the Sabbath Day or it would be considered work, which, of course you can't do on that day. Also, you can't walk very far on the Sabbath or you will exceed the limits of a Sabbath Day's journey. Jehovah's law has so many rules that I can't even remember them all, but if you break one of them, you're in trouble." After a brief pause she added, "you can't think for yourself but you must always hearken to the voice of Jehovah. There is a lot more freedom in worshipping Baal. I just couldn't take all those rules."

"I didn't know that it was that bad," stated Rachel.

Gomer continued her onslaught against Jehovah worship. "Jehovah doesn't promise His worshippers anything that Baal doesn't promise, except with Baal, you don't have to live such a stringent lifestyle. I don't know why people can't see that," she concluded.

"What about Hosea, did he treat you badly?" enquired Bianca.

"No, I can't say that he did, but, he listened to Jehovah all the time. We couldn't make any decisions for ourselves, Jehovah made them all. He even named our three children. With each birth I had a name picked out but I could never use it. Jehovah picked out the names."

"What did your husband think of that?" asked Hannah. Bianca was glad she asked the question so she wouldn't have to make her feelings so obvious by asking about Hosea.

"He just kept telling me that we had no choice but to obey Jehovah."

"But he did love you, didn't he? Hosea did love you," asked Sarah.

"Yeah, I guess so. He didn't make much money as a prophet of Jehovah but, all in all, I think he loved me."

"You guess so...you think so! What's the matter with you?" exploded Bianca. "The fact that he married you proves that he loves you. Do you think anyone else would do the same thing? No matter what Jehovah said, there isn't another man in Israel that would look twice at you. Gomer, I think you are just a spoiled brat who doesn't know when she is well off."

"That's easy for you to say," replied Gomer. "You didn't have to live like that."

"I don't see that it was that terrible," countered Bianca. "So your husband didn't make much money. It doesn't look like you came back here in rags. He certainly didn't deprive you. Hosea always was crazy about you and would do anything for you."

"Did you know him?" asked Gomer. "Did you know my husband?"

"Yes, I knew him, but I don't think you ever did. You didn't even know your own husband. If you did you would never say 'I guess so,' when asked about his love."

"I lived with him for years," responded Gomer. "I think I know him."

"You can live with someone and not really know them, you know," concluded Bianca. "Look, I'm leaving so you don't have to concern yourself with my opinion." Bianca stood to go. "But before I go I just want to make my thoughts clear. You didn't know your husband and that lack of knowledge has destroyed your marriage and will destroy you." Having spoken her piece, Bianca stood to leave. Before she reached the door, Gomer called to her.

"Bianca, wait, please. You said you knew my husband. Have you spoken to him lately? Please, tell me."

"Spoken to him? No, I've never spoken to him. I just, sort of knew who he was."

"She used to like him," said Hannah.

"Thanks a lot, Hannah," spoke Bianca, with plenty of sarcasm. "Alright, I'll admit it. I used to carry the torch for Hosea while he carried the torch for you. He didn't know that I existed any more than you knew that he existed. So, no, I haven't spoken to him."

"That's strange," replied Gomer.

"That I never talked to him?" asked Bianca.

No," answered a bewildered Gomer. "It is what you said about lack of knowledge destroying me. You told me the same thing that Hosea tells people in his preaching. He is always saying that 'there is no knowledge of God in the land.' Or sometimes he says 'my people are destroyed for lack of knowledge.' Then other times he will say that 'my people have rejected knowledge,' that's knowledge of God, of course. I just thought it was strange the way you spoke of lack of knowledge destroying me, just the way Hosea speaks of it destroying God's people."

Everyone was silent for a moment, considering this strange coincidence. It seemed to be an eerie moment for everyone. Finally, Rachel broke the silence and lightened up the moment. "Maybe Bianca is a prophetess," she said. They all laughed. "Wouldn't that be something? One of Baal's girls is a prophetess of Jehovah."

"I'm no prophetess," protested Bianca. "I don't know why I worded that phrase the way I did. I just told the truth about how I feel. If I offended you, Gomer, I'm sorry. But that's how I see it, and I would see it that way whether I cared anything about Hosea or not."

"Still, you have to admit that it is uncanny how you used the same phrase as a person whom you haven't even talked with," stated Hannah. "It makes you feel kind of creepy."

Sarah spoke up and said, "I know what it is. You are so in love with Hosea that you a mentally joined together. I've heard of stuff like this. Even though you can never be together physically, you have mentally come together."

"You've mentally come apart, is what I think," was Bianca's cutting reply. "It was just a coincidence, that's all. I don't know why you are making such a big deal over it."

"Seriously though," interjected Rachel, "the fact that you said the same words as Hosea could prove that they are true. I mean, you don't have to be a prophetess for Jehovah to cause you to say something."

"That's how I see it," replied Hannah. What do you think, Gomer?"

"Frankly girls, at this time, I'd rather not think about it. Don't leave, Bianca. Stay. Everyone stay and have some lunch."

At that moment the subject was permanently changed. Nothing more was said about why Gomer left Hosea, Bianca's love for Hosea or the strange remark that she made. The girls had lunch and enjoyed one another's company.

CHAPTER SIX

"Why can't I live here with you?" Jezreel's question hung in the air like a threatening storm cloud. Gomer was beginning to think that allowing him to come and visit was a mistake. She wanted to see her children so bad, that her heart leapt in her chest when she heard that he had come to visit. Normally minors were not allowed in the compound without parental accompaniment, but they allowed his visit since it was her child. She was, in fact, the only one of Baal's girls that had a family, so, his visit was rather unusual.

When he asked to leave his father and live with her, she knew that she must not allow it. Yet, how do you explain to a nine year old why he could not live there on the temple grounds with her and the other of Baal's girls. "Because it's not permitted," she explained in half- truth.

"But you said yourself that the other women don't have any children. Besides, if I am to be a Priest of Baal someday, where could I get better training?"

"Honey, look around. Do you see any other children your age?" She paused when he didn't answer and added, "If I could have you with me, I would, but I can't."

"Just tell me why," he demanded. "Why can't children be here with their own parents?" He had her trapped and she knew it. There was no way that she could explain to him all of the aspects of Baal worship. He was too young to understand it. She was not even sure he understood anything about the man and woman relationship, let alone how it functioned in her religion.

Her mind quickly scanned the facts about Baalism to see if there was any way to explain it to a child. They believed that if a married couple was having difficulty conceiving a child, the man could be with one of Baal's girls and in doing so, it would empower his fertility. The wife could do the same with a priest of Baal with the same result. Gomer could not find any way to explain that to her son. "It's just against the rules," she finally concluded.

This explanation was totally unacceptable to Jezreel. He knew that she was being completely honest with him. He didn't know why, but he could not tolerate it. "You just don't want me," he exploded. He got up and hurried toward the door. She called after him but he would not stop or look back. He left her staring at a door that he had slammed behind him.

Tears streamed down his cheeks as he raced for home. He hoped that he would not encounter any friends on his way home because he knew that his emotions would not permit him to stop and it would be hard to explain afterwards. What he did not know as he sped along was that for every tear he shed, his mother was shedding another one back where he left her.

After entering his own front door, he slammed that one too. Fortunately, Father was out back and too far away to hear the door slamming. Otherwise, Jezreel would have to give an explanation and that was something that he definitely didn't want to do.

Only Rahumah and Ammi were in the house at the time. They both were startled at his entrance and continued to gaze at him for a few moments afterward. Finally Rahumah spoke, "did you see momma?"

"Yes, I saw her," he groaned.

"You don't seem very happy about it," she answered.

"You sound like you got sand in your throat," added Ammi. Rahumah smiled but Jezreel didn't seem to think it was funny. He turned away as if he was going to leave the room, but he stopped and dropped into a large chair.

"She doesn't want me. She doesn't want any of us."

"What do you mean, 'she doesn't want us'?" asked Rahumah.

"I asked if I could live with her, okay?" The two younger children stood in silent amazement. "She said no," he continued. "This is great! First, Father drives her away and now she doesn't want us."

"Father didn't drive her away," protested Ammi.

Jezreel continued to complain as if he didn't even hear Ammi. "I even told her that I wanted to be a priest of Baal, thinking that would persuade her, but she still said I couldn't live there." He looked out the window at his father who was weeding in the garden. "He did drive her away, Ammi. He was always saying that Jehovah wanted this or Jehovah wanted that. He left her with no choices. She didn't want to yield to Jehovah's every whim, so he drove her away".

Not knowing what to say, both of the younger children remained silent. "You were both too young. I'm older. I remember how it was." He turned to his two siblings and said," They were always arguing and I heard them. Father always wanted to do what Jehovah wanted and Mother didn't. He would never compromise and that's what drove her away."

"Do you still want to be a priest of Baal," asked Rahumah. She knew that she was slightly changing the subject.

"I know one thing, I'll never be a prophet of Jehovah," was his noncommittal answer. As he turned around, he noticed his father standing in the doorway. How long he was there, Jezreel didn't know, but it was obvious that he heard his last remark. Perhaps he had heard even more. In anger, Jezreel said no more but raced to his bedroom and shut the door.

"He's mad," explained Ammi.

"I know he is," replied Hosea. "I know that he blames me for his mother leaving." He had a haggard look on his face. It was so frustrating to know what to do about his situation, if there was anything he could do. As a prophet, it was his duty to be always obedient to Jehovah. This, he felt was a life for a single man, not one who is married. Yet, Jehovah had told him to get married and now he was left with this confusing, heartbreaking situation.

"He says that he will never be a prophet, like you," said Rahumah.

"Yes, I heard him. I understand his anger, but, in a way, he is a prophet whether he likes it or not. His name is a reminder that Jehovah will bring King Jehu down from his throne because of his sin."

"What does his name mean?" asked Rahumah.

"His name means, 'Jehovah will disperse' or Jehovah will sow by scattering seeds'." replied her father. "Jehovah will scatter Jehu's kingdom and sow another one it it's place."

"Why?" asked Ammi.

"Well, King Jehu had sown some very bad seed in his reign and now it must be uprooted."

"You mean he planted a bad garden?" asked Ammi.

"In a way, he did. In all of our actions we are planting seed. If we plant bad seed we will have a bad harvest. We must sow seeds of righteousness and we will reap God's mercy." Hosea sensed that Jehovah was speaking through him even as he spoke to his children. "Sowing bad seed is like scattering seed to the wind. When we do that we reap a whirlwind of problems."

"Wow," exclaimed Ammi.

"That's neat," added Rahumah. "I want to always do good things, so my seed will grow good things."

"That's the best thing to do," Hosea stated, affirming her determination.

Later, as Hosea was working in his garden, Hosea was thinking about the answers that he had given the children. He knew that they were the words that Jehovah had given him. He would have to remember them to speak them in the king's court. Then he thought of his angry son, Jezreel and the ever present heartache returned. It seemed that it was never gone for long.

CHAPTER SEVEN

Dibliam stood outside the temple staring at the edifice with the shinny exterior and high obelisks. His first response was to think of this heathen structure as an affront to Jehovah and he immediately felt outraged. Then, as he thought on it, he began to see the temple as a large tombstone, representing the spiritual death of all the followers of Baal. Either way, he resented having to even enter the temple and to proceed through it to the temple grounds.

When he was younger, he would never have entered such a place. It was not even worthy of his presence. He had not visited Gomer the first time she became one of Baal's girls. He was younger and prouder at that time and he had hoped that she would come to her senses and leave. Marrying a prophet and leaving Baal's service was like a dream come true. It was beyond anything he could even ask for or think of.

His mind drifted back to the day Gomer was born. He and his wife were so happy. Immediately they were both filled with such hope and lofty dreams for their daughter. They resolved to give her every advantage that they could afford to assure her future. They purposed to introduce her to young men from the finest families that they knew. That was their dream. How had it all gone wrong?

Even when Gomer was very young, she didn't seem to be interested in her parents' dreams for her. She never liked the young men that they had picked out for her. Her interests always seemed to go to the guys that her parents would not like. They were young men who could never give her a comfortable, respectable living. Watching her chase after these fellows broke their hearts.

The older Gomer became, the more distant from her parents she seemed to grow. Then the arguments began. She accused her parents of trying to run and ruin her life. She kept saying that she had rights and she had her own dreams that she intended to follow. She was bored with the boys that they had picked out for her and could never be happy with them. Over and over, the same arguments were repeated and they were never resolved.

Then, the unthinkable happened. Dibliam's wife died. It had happened very sudden. One day she was there and the next day she was gone. Dibliam was so shocked and so heartbroken that he did not have the strength to debate with Gomer. She pretty well did what she wanted to do, while he stayed home wishing that he had died with his wife. Did Gomer even miss her mother? He couldn't tell.

One day Gomer left the house and was gone for three or four days. Her father did not know it at the time, but she had been at the temple of Baal. When she returned home, she announced to her father that she was leaving home and was going to be a temple harlot and serve Baal. Not knowing what to say he probably reacted in the worst way he could. He told his daughter that if she did such a thing that she was no longer his daughter and he would neither visit her nor invite her to his home. Unfazed by her father's threats, she left anyway.

Now Dibliam was experiencing compounded grief. First, he grieved for his wife, and also for his daughter. He was only glad that his wife was not there to witness their daughter's decent into wickedness.

He decided that he had spent enough time gathering wool and proceeded toward the door. Soon he found himself seated in his daughter's apartment across the room from her. She had greeted him pleasantly enough even though she could not conceal her tentativeness. She wasn't sure whether or not to expect a renewal of one of their arguments.

"So, how have you been?" her father asked her.

As tempted as she was to tell him that she knew that he did not come to inquire about her health and to reveal the hypocrisy of his question, she politely responded by saying "fine, thank you." She did not enquire about his well-being but, instead awaited the real purpose of his visit to be revealed. A long, uncomfortable pause followed their initial exchange.

"I visited Hosea and saw the children," he offered. She nodded but gave no response. "It was good to see them," he continued. This time she said nothing without even nodding her head. "The children miss you terribly."

"And you are wondering if I won't come home to them right? I hate it when you beat around the bush like you do. Why can't you ever just come out and say what is on your mind?" She couldn't keep the sarcasm out of her voice or the bitterness from her expression.

"Well, you are their mother," he countered. "Would you have liked it if your mother had left home when you were a little child?"

"It's not the same thing," she shouted back at him. "Mother was your wife and my mother and that's all she was."

"Weren't you the same thing to Hosea and the children?"

"Yes, I was those things and if that's all I was it would have been fine. But I had to be more than that. Don't forget I was married to a prophet of Jehovah."

"So what? Is there something wrong with being the wife of a prophet?"

In response to this remark, Gomer threw her hands up in the air. "You don't get it, do you?" she asked her father. "You simply don't get it."

"No," he countered, "I guess I don't get it. A lot of girls would love to be a wife of a prophet. Many girls thought that you had it lucky."

"Lucky? She asked. That word seemed to fuel the fire that was in her to burn even brighter. "They thought I was lucky? Let them try being a wife to one of Jehovah's prophets." With a burning resolve that had been bottled up inside her for a long time, she looked her father straight in the eyes and sardonically said, "If you are the wife to one of those prophets you are not just a wife and mother, you get to be one of Jehovah's slaves." The shocked expression on Dibliam's face was the exact result that Gomer had hoped to achieve. She confidently sat back and with her expression challenged him to answer that statement, if he could.

After he recovered from her shocking remark, he finally muttered, "Why, that's crazy. I know of a lot of prophets and their wives don't feel like slaves."

"That's because they don't know any other way. They grew up worshipping Jehovah." He could not answer this because the same was true of him and his late wife. Jehovah worship was all they knew, but they always found it satisfying. They never even thought of trying anything else. She seemed to be reading his thoughts, because next she stated, "And what about you and mother? You staunchly worshipped Jehovah. You don't know the freedom that comes from worshipping Baal."

"Freedom?" he asked.

"Yes, freedom, and look at all the benefits." Gomer had gained momentum by now, as if she were on a wagon riding down a steep hill. "I have rooms full of corn, wine and oil. I have been given silver and gold. Where do you suppose it comes from? It must come from worshippers of Baal who freely give to me, one of His girls."

Dibliam could only gaze at her as she smugly sat gazing at him knowing that he had no reply. The truth was that he did have a reply but was forbidden to give it. He knew that Hosea had been the one supporting her, but he did not know that he had been so extravagant. He virtually had to bit his tongue to keep from telling her the truth. If he was allowed to respond to her as he could and would like to, it would take the wind out of her sails. Instead he had to remain silent because he had promised Hosea that he would not tell her.

"You can't answer that, can you, Father?" She had not called him 'Father' in a very long time. Under these circumstances, however, it brought him no satisfaction.

"Let me just tell you this," he replied, "You don't know you're husband." Before she could give him another cutting reply, he continued, "Oh, I know that you think you do. In some ways you know him better than anyone else, but there is a side of him that you don't really know. And what's worse, everybody can see it but you."

Gone was the confident smile from her face. Her mind shot back to an earlier conversation when Bianca had told her the same thing.

Bianca and her father did not even know each other. How could they both say the same thing when they hadn't even consulted each other? All she could ever see was how restricting life with Hosea had been. What was it that she didn't know about him.

"I think that you should leave now, Father," she quietly replied. She needed time to ponder these coincidental comments.

"I suppose you are right," he sighed. "We're certainly not getting anywhere." He stood to leave but stood and thoughtfully stared into space. "You know what I was thinking about as I was walking over here? I was thinking about when you were born."

"Oh please, let's not go through that," she pleaded as she was shaking her head. She purposefully tried to sound as condescending as possible.

"Alright, alright," he reluctantly agreed. "No trip down memory lane. But I will say that your mother was the happiest woman alive on that day. I can't help wondering, do you miss her at all?"

"Well, certainly I miss her. What kind of a question is that?"

"Well, from the time she died you have never spoken of her. I've never seen you crying. You don't give any indication that you do miss her."

"Well, she and I were different. We never agreed on anything. We just didn't see eye to eye on many different subjects."

"So, you are relieved that she is gone," he concluded. She started to say something but remained silent instead. "You don't miss your mother or your husband. Both of whom loved you very much. I don't think that you knew either one of them. And although you are my daughter and I love you but I don't think I know you either." Without another word from either of them, Dibliam departed. There were tears in his eyes as he exited the temple and entered the street, these were tears that his daughter would never see. She probably wouldn't even care that she had brought him pain. She resented Jehovah. She didn't love her mother or her husband and kids. Who was this woman who, as a girl grew up in his house? Is this the child that had sat on his knee and looked up adoringly at him? How did everything that had promised to always be right become so wrong?

He thought for a moment of visiting Hosea and reporting on his visit to Gomer, but he didn't have the strength to go through it again. There was nothing left for him to do but go back home and mourn his losses. Perhaps Jehovah meant for him to share in the heartbreak that Hosea spoke about. Is this how heartbroken that God is about the rebellion of His people? If so, then Dibliam understood a little bit how God was feeling that day. As devastated as he was personally, he resolved to do his best to live in a way that would never add to that sorrow.

Suddenly it started to lightly rain. The wet drops on his face startled him at first. Speaking to God, Dibliam said "Of course! I know why it's raining. You're mingling your tears with mine, aren't you Father?" Comforted just a little bit with his realization he thanked his Heavenly Father as he trudged the lonely street and proceeded for home.

CHAPTER EIGHT

"Who was that man visiting you," asked Rachel. "I know that it is none of my business and I'm being as nosy as all get out, but I hope you will tell me."

"Why?" answered Gomer. "Why do you want to know?"

"Because," answered Rachel.

"That's not an answer," insisted Gomer.

"Because I'm busting with curiosity and if you don't tell me I'll just explode into a million pieces." They both had to laugh at Rachel's frank admission. "Then it will be your fault that I'm gone and you'll be sorry."

"Well, I sure don't want that to happen so I'll tell you. It was my father, that's who it was."

"Oh," was all that Rachel uttered. "That's not a good sign."

"Why not?"

"Usually when fathers visit one of Baal's girls it's to give her bad news. Some family member died or some old boyfriend is just pining away without her. Only, in your case it would probably be your husband who is doing the pining."

"Do we have to discuss this right now?" pleaded Gomer. "I'm too tired."

"You're not tired, you're upset," perceived Rachel. "He must have said something to upset you." She didn't ask what it was that had upset Gomer, but she hoped she would tell her.

"I'll tell you, I promise, but later. Okay?"

"Okay, as long as you promise," conceded Rachel. "Why don't we get the other girls and go for a walk. Maybe it will make you feel better. You always seem invigorated after a good brisk walk."

As it turned out, Sarah was too busy for a walk but the other girls were eager to go. They too had noticed that Gomer had a visitor and were no less curious than Rachel was. At first, nobody spoke. Each was hoping that Gomer would volunteer her information. She noticed them glancing at her, but tried to ignore them. When she found this to be impossible, she finally opened up.

"Hannah, Bianca, I'm going to tell you the same thing that I told Rachel, I will tell you about my father's visit later. I'm too tired to talk about it now."

"Okay, we can wait," answered Bianca.

"You don't have to bite our heads off," contributed Hannah. "You can't blame us for wondering. I think you would wonder, too, if one of us had a mysterious visitor."

"I didn't mean to bite your head off. And he wasn't all that mysterious, he was my father."

"Hey, what's going on over there?" Rachel asked, pointing toward a large crowd of people.

"It looks like somebody is selling something," answered Bianca. "Let's go and see what it is."

When the ladies arrived at the place and joined the crowd, they discovered that it was a slave market. People were selling other human beings. The four of them were all astounded at what was going on there. They watched in shocking amazement as each pathetic person was marched up onto the platform and forced to be humiliated before the crowd of people. Some of the poor victims were compelled to undress in front of the crowd of buyers. Others had their teeth checked or their heads checked for lice. Gomer's heart went out to each one and the others seemed in silent agreement. All four of them were quietly thankful that they were not among the wretched lot that was sold that day. For some reason, none of the women could force themselves to move but they were transfixed until the sale was completed.

Just as the crowd was about to leave, a voice cried, "Wait, we have one more to sell." Again they all watched as an older woman was walked into position. Like all the others, she stood with her head bowed, awaiting her miserable fate.

"Hey," Gomer called, "Isn't that one of Baal's servants? You know the one who lived across the way from Sarah?"

"Yeah, that's old Esther," responded Hannah.

"Why is she being sold as a slave?" asked Rachel. A long silence followed the unanswered question. Each girl was locked into her own horrified thoughts. Finally, Bianca asked a question that they were all wondering about.

"How can she be sold as a slave, when we have Baal who is supposed to protect us?" she asked.

"Maybe she sinned against Baal or something," countered Hannah.

"Yeah," replied Bianca, "That must be it."

"You are probably right," countered Rachel. "She must have done something wrong."

"What else could it be?" added Gomer.

The four women continued to walk as they dropped back into troubled silence. Again and again they repeated their conclusion but they were always unsuccessful in relieving their quiet fears. Finally, Gomer asked the question that they were all afraid to face.

"Do you think that…" she hesitated for a moment before speaking her fears out loud. No one else would finish the question for her, so she continued. "Do you think that, you know, this might happen to us one day?"

"Never,"

"Certainly not, it could never happen to us."

"Why would you ask that?"

"Well," Gomer replied in trepidation, "it could be that Esther sinned or maybe she was sold because she was old." After walking a little further, she further asked, "What does happen to the older members of our group? There doesn't seem to be any around the temple."

"They go to the retirement place," answered Hannah.

"Where's that?" asked Gomer. "Has anybody seen it?" There came no immediate answer from any of the girls. "How do we know that they didn't all end up at the slave market?"

Bianca answered, "Gomer, you're getting all worked up over nothing. We're never going to be sold as slaves." Bianca was trying to muster up as much courage as she could, to convince herself as well as the others. "Besides, if we did get sold, we could always be redeemed or set free at the Jubilee."

Finally, somebody said something that relieved their worries. They had forgotten about the Jewish custom of redemption, in which a relative could buy back the freedom of someone sold into slavery. The Jubilee also gave them hope. On the fiftieth year, all slaves were set free. It wasn't quite as promising as the hope of redemption, but gave them some assurance. Everyone's countenance brightened considerably.

"That's right," agreed Gomer. "I forgot all about those things." The women began to smile and laugh as they proceeded on their walk. Soon that they almost forgot about the horrible slave market and the poor victims being sold.

Eventually Bianca spoke up and said, "Okay Gomer. Now that I have relieved your mind, it is time for you to relieve ours."

"How am I supposed to do that?" she asked.

"Tell us about your father's visit." Bianca couldn't help giggling as she spoke. Soon the other girls were laughing and concurring with Bianca.

"Okay! Okay! I can see that you will never quit bugging me until I tell you, so here goes. He came to try to persuade me to return to my husband. That's all there is to it. There is nothing mysterious about it. So, I'm sorry to disappoint you, but it was nothing more than that."

"Wait a minute," protested Rachel, "he said something to upset you, I could tell."

"What was it?" questioned Hannah. "What did he say?" Gomer was reluctant to answer, so they proceeded along their way in silence. All three of her companions looked at Gomer as they walked along the road.

"You may as well tell us because we are going to bother you until you do," said Rachel.

Finally gomer complied, "He said...he said the same thing you said, Bianca."

"What did I say?" a baffled Bianca replied.

"Remember, the other night you said that I didn't know Hosea?"

"Yeah, that's what he said?"

"So," answered Rachel, "what's so terrible about that?"

"It's as if Bianca and my father had rehearsed it or something." The others continued to stare at her in bewilderment. "Don't you see? I know that they couldn't have done that. They don't even know each other. It just gave me the weirdest feeling, that's all. I still get creepy just thinking about it. It's like a de-je-vu thing or something." No one said anything for a few minutes. Finally, gomer asked, "Well, wouldn't that make you wonder?"

Everyone agreed that what had happened was strange, but no one offered an explanation. The walk that promised to refresh and invigorate them had only served to burden their minds with heavy thoughts. First was the slave sale and then Gomer's strange experience. Finally, Gomer broke the silence. "Well, somebody say something. What do you think of my weird father and his strange statement?"

"Well, off hand, I'd say that somebody was trying to tell you something," offered Bianca.

"Sounds that way to me too," agreed Rachel. They all looked at Hannah and she merely nodded in agreement.

"What, you mean like Jehovah is speaking to me? It can't be Baal. He wouldn't tell me to leave His service." Gomer pondered the concept some more. Finally, she concluded, "No I can't believe that. That's crazy!"

"Well then," asked Bianca, "what do you make of it?"

"It's just a weird coincidence. You know how fathers can make you feel goofy things." This they all had to agree with. "And my father is the weirdest of them all. I mean, he's way out there."

"Well, this whole day has got us keyed up," agreed Rachel.

"Maybe we ought to head for home," said Bianca.

"...before something else spooky happens," concluded Hannah.

"I don't think I can take anything more," asserted Gomer. The others agreed and they did an about face and started back. Nothing more was said about the slave sale or Gomer's father.

When gomer was alone again, she tried to busy herself with chores in an effort to occupy her mind. However, as much as she tried to forget her troublesome experiences, she could not. First, her father had her unnerved and then they had to run across that terrible slave sale. As much as she hated to admit it to herself, that slave sale and the looks of hopeless terror on the faces of the slaves had really gotten to her.

Poor Esther! What could have she done that was so terrible? She always seemed like such a pleasant person. In fact, Gomer always wondered how she could smile as much as she did. It seemed that she was never depressed or sad about anything. Now she was. She certainly wasn't smiling when Gomer seen her being sold.

The thing that troubled Gomer the most was the nagging fear that what she had witnessed happening to Esther could one day happen to her. Again and again she reminded herself of the possibility of redemption or being set free at the Jubilee. Again and again she had to fight back the same fears that brutally forced themselves into her mind. Then she would remind herself of the power of Baal and that He would never allow such a miserable thing to happen to one of His girls. This also failed to bring her peace.

As she extinguished the lamp that night, her mental battle was still rampaging. Troubled, she laid awake for a long time. Finally, she fell into a quiet, fitful sleep.

CHAPTER NINE

Just as Hosea had opened the door, he was surprised to see his friend, Amos, who was about to knock on the outside. Both of the prophets were startled by their unexpected encounter. Hosea was determined to make an unannounced visit to the Temple of Baal. Amos had come to visit a friend.

"Are you going somewhere?" Amos asked his fellow prophet.

"Yes," he answered. He pondered whether it was wise share his intentions with Amos. Even though Amos had been his one true blue friend throughout this whole ordeal, Hosea knew that he did not fully understand his feelings.

"Let me guess, you're going to the temple, right?"

"Why do you say that?"

"If it was a trip to the market or some other such errand, you would have been forth coming with the information. You hesitated, that's how I knew."

Hosea just sighed and said nothing for a moment. Finally, he said, "I've got to do something. I'll go crazy if I don't." Amos nodded in silence. Hosea continued, "You don't know what it is like for me. The kids don't even ask about their mother any more, they just look at me, silently pleading with me to make things right somehow. When I pass people on the street they cease their conversation and look at me like I was a thing to be pitied. If I don't do something, I'll go crazy."

"But, what do you hope to accomplish? You couldn't keep her from leaving. What makes you think you can convince her to return?" Amos' argument was perfectly logical, but Hosea was not in a logical frame of mind. Frankly, he was desperate.

"I know…I know what you are saying and it makes sense but…"

"But you feel like you have to try something."

"Don't you see, if there is the slightest chance of getting her back, I have to try it?"

Amos could see that he was not making any progress with his present line of argument, so he tried another approach. "Hosea, Jehovah told you to marry Gomer so that your marriage would serve as an object lesson to the people. I know that it's painful to you, but so far it has played out perfectly. By watching your grief and heartache, people can see how their wicked ways have affected Jehovah."

Hosea had to admit to himself that he had temporarily forgotten his mission. In his despair he could only think about how painful his life had been. "Well, I don't think I'm a very good example of Jehovah."

"Oh, I think you are a perfect example of Jehovah. If you weren't hurting, how would the people know how Jehovah's heart is breaking over their sins?"

"I guess you're right. What you said makes me think of something little Ammi told me back when Gomer first left home. He said, 'Jehovah must be awful sad'."

"And he's right. You know he is."

"I know, I know! I just wish…I don't know what I wish."

"You wish the pain would go away," answered Amos. "I can't blame you there, and it hurts to see you go through this, but, it is Jehovah's assignment and like all other prophets you must see it through."

After Amos left, Hosea had found a temporary resolve to do nothing about the situation. Then he got to telling himself that Jehovah would do anything to get His people back and so he rationalized that he would be justified in doing the same. Again, he decided to visit the temple and talk to Gomer.

Word had spread throughout the temple grounds that Gomer's husband had come to visit. Everyone knew about it and everyone seemed to have an opinion about it. Some believed he had come to compel her to come home. Others thought that he had come to make her an offer that would be too good to resist. Then there were those who believed he had come to beg her and she would cave in, unable to refuse him.

When Gomer heard that he was coming, she just sighed. As curious as her friends were about her father's visit, she knew that their curiosity would be out of control now. Yet, there was no way she could prevent him from coming, so she decided to brace herself and go through with it.

He looked haggard and very unhappy as he walked through her door. For a brief moment, her heart almost went out to him. However, her mind quickly returned to how unjustly she had been treated by him and his God and the old feelings of anger returned. They were both awkward in each other's presence at first. Both made an attempt at small talk and both failed.

Finally in exasperation Hosea said "Gomer, I miss you. The kids miss you. Couldn't you come home and make one more effort?" Gomer surprised herself with how angry she was at his inevitable request.

"Does your God miss me too?" she asked, unable to keep the sharp sarcasm out of her tone.

"Gomer, you don't mean that, you can't," he defensively said.

"You give up that domineering God of yours and I'll come home," she further demanded. "Serve Baal, Hosea, He is a god of freedom, not like that dictator you serve." When she said that, his shoulders slumped in defeat. He could plainly see that his friend, Amos was right. There was no persuading her to return. Yet, this was his only chance, he had to keep trying.

"Couldn't you come home for the children's sake. Rahumah and Ammi miss you terribly and Jezreel is becoming more of a problem every day. He barely speaks to me and he doesn't speak to his brother or sister very much."

"No," she quickly replied. "I will not return home to live in those unbearable circumstances. Not now. Not ever." There was a long, silent pause. Hosea had run out of arguments. He desperately wished that he could think of another one, but, he couldn't. Finally Gomer said, "I think that it is best that you leave now, and please, don't come back". Utterly defeated, he started for the door.

He paused before exiting and said, "I won't come back here, unless you ask me to."

"That, I will never do," she answered. Without looking back, he exited the door closing it behind him. Staring at the door, Gomer was thinking of how his visit wasn't too bad. When her friends asked her, her answers would be direct and simple. She wasn't prepared for what was going to happen next.

Hosea walked toward the exit of the temple grounds, feeling like a complete failure. Yet, as he walked along, he felt the Spirit of God moving inside of him and he knew that he was about to give a prophecy. He recognized the feeling from the other times that Jehovah had given him some message to give to his people.

As Hosea reached the gate, he turned and faced the temple yard. Some of Baal's girls were milling about, as well as some people who frequented the temple. They were all startled when Hosea began to raise his voice. Gomer could hear the commotion from her place and groaned inwardly. Everybody would know about this. She couldn't select certain parts of Hosea's visit and tell it. The whole embarrassing scene was played out for all to see and hear.

"Oh Israel," he began," return unto the Lord thy God; for thou hast fallen by your iniquity. For the Lord has a controversy with the inhabitants of the land, because there is no truth, nor mercy, nor knowledge of the Lord in the land. However, you can know Him by following on to know the Lord."

Some people shook their heads and walked away and others listened. Some seemed to be too shocked to do anything but stare at the prophet as if he were accosting them personally.

"Because you have sown to the wind, you will reap the whirlwind," Hosea continued. "Israel has forgotten his maker. Israel is an empty vine and a backslidden heifer. Yet Jehovah invites you to return to Him. If you do, he promises to heal your backsliding and love you freely. Listen, people, sow to yourselves in righteousness and you'll reap in mercy. Break up the fallow ground of your heart, for it is time to seek the Lord until He come and rain righteousness upon you. "

Some of the priests of Baal had gathered together to determine what to do about this dreadful event. All agreed that this crazy prophet must be silenced, but how? They decided to get all the priests and temple guards. By ganging up on him, force him to leave the temple area.

Hosea saw them coming but did not stop speaking. He decided to prophecy until he was physical forced to stop. He noticed a young woman who looked vaguely familiar at the edge of the crowd. She seemed to be listening to him and Hosea sensed that she wanted to talk to him. However, he could not stop and invite a conversation because he knew that he had little time to speak to the people.

"Jehovah promises to be as dew unto Israel and the people will grow as a lily. His anger will be turned away if you will return to Him." As the priests approached Hosea, he concluded, "who is wise and he shall understand these things. If you are prudent, you will know that the ways of the Lord are right and the just shall walk in them."

Just then, he was seized by the guards and they proceeded to escort him out the door. Out of the corner of his eye, Hosea noticed the young lady who was listening to him begin to follow the gang of priests and guards.

"Don't you come back here," one of the priests ordered. "You will not be allowed in the gate. We keep troublemakers like you out." So Hosea was left outside the gate, as the priests and their entourage went back inside. Yet the young woman, who had followed him out stood there with him.

"You look familiar," he confessed. "Do I know you?"

"I'm Bianca. I went to school with you and Gomer," she answered.

"I remember your face, but I don't know if I ever knew your name. Did you want to talk to me?"

Bianca moved closer. She seemed to be struggling to find the words to express what she wanted to say. "You came here to get Gomer, didn't you? I mean…what other reason would you have for being here?"

"Yes, I came for her. But she refused me." He was struggling to hold back the tears. He no longer felt the strong inspiration that he felt as he spoke the words of God just a short time ago. "All those things I said about Israel refusing Jehovah, is exactly how she refused me."

Unsure how to open the subject that she wanted to speak of,

Bianca took a few minutes to work up her nerve. Hosea still hadn't given her much thought because his mind was still on Gomer, his speech and the rude expulsion that the priests had given him. Finally he began to wonder why this woman had approached him and started to look at her with a questioning stare.

Bianca knew that she had to start talking so she began with a question. "Does it have to be Gomer who leaves with you?" She could see that her question didn't make any sense, she plunged ahead. "I mean…I know that you came for Gomer and I think she is foolish for not going with you. Well, what I'm trying to say is wouldn't another woman do just as well as her? I know that you are a lonely man and you have children at home who need a mother and…well, their real mother won't go to them. So, I wonder if you had given any thought to…ah…a second choice." Bianca knew that she was babbling now, but she couldn't help herself. Despising her own nervousness, she forced herself to get to the point. "What I'm trying to say is, I would be willing to come with you and be your wife, if Gomer refuses."

Hosea stared at her in shocking amazement. Certainly he had never considered anything this woman was suggesting and he wasn't sure how to answer her. The woman he loved was refusing to be with him and here was someone else offering herself to him in brazen forwardness.

"Did you say your name was Bianca?"

"Yes."

"Well, Bianca I…ah…I don't know what to say. I mean I just met you and…I don't know. I never thought or …did anything like you are suggesting. I can't imagine being with anyone but Gomer."

"But, you would never be sorry. I'd be everything you would want in a wife and more."

When Bianca first started talking to him, he was surprised and unsure of his own feelings. Now, he was convinced that no one could replace Gomer for him. It was her or no one. "I'm sorry, Bianca but I have to have her. No one else will do."

Bianca was desperate now. She felt like she was laying herself out for the buzzards. Her pride was totally abased. She felt she had to convince him to take her on any circumstances. "I don't know why you want her. She never loved you."

"What do you mean? How could you know that?"

"I went to school with you, remember? I used to watch you as you couldn't take your eyes off of her. Foolishly, I hoped, that you would glance my way…just once. But you never did. And now, you turn your back on the one who loves you for the one who doesn't."

"I'm sorry," he lamented. I never knew…"

"Of course you never knew, how could you? You had tunnel vision for her." Her tears were falling freely and she hated herself for letting him see her cry. "Oh I'm pathetic, I know it. I've abased myself to the very dust and still you despise me." After a brief silence, she said, "Well, I guess I better go." And she turned to depart. She started walking toward the gate that would take her back to the life that she hoped to leave. She heard him saying something that sounded like an apology, but she couldn't respond. She could only take so much humiliation for one day.

As she entered the gate, she felt that the eyes of the entire temple community was upon her. Surely everyone knew why she had talked to Hosea. It was obvious that he refused her. There was no way that she could hide that. Her tears wouldn't stop flowing and she hated every one of them. She felt as if she was stripped of any pride or dignity and that she was walking home naked and that everyone could see her.

Did they think of her as amusing? Did they find her to be pathetic? All of her wishes, fantasies and dreams had just gone up in smoke. The man who she had wished for all of her life had humiliated her to the very dust. Never could she hold her head up in public again. The mere shell of the woman that she once had been, made her way home. She went inside and shut the door and wished that she would never have to open it again.

CHAPTER TEN

Gomer was furious. How could he come here and pull such a stunt? Every reason that she had for leaving him in the first place, he just magnified ten times as much. She was glad that he had been expelled and told to never return. She only wished that the priests had done even more to hurt him, if they could. She thought about what she had said to him when he was here. She hoped that her words stung like hornets. If they didn't, she wished that she could have thought of something nastier to say.

How could she face her friends? Oh, they would be around, probably within a half hour. What had ever possessed her to marry this man in the first place? Maybe if she had married another man, even a worshipper of Jehovah, but certainly not a prophet. One could never tell when they went into a frenzy and proclaimed things that embarrassed a person like her to tears.

Gomer had watched Bianca chase after him. Her shameless act certainly was not surprizing. Yet she did not stick around to watch her friend's abasement. She was too embarrassed and angry. If Bianca wanted to make a fool out of herself, that was her business. Why should Gomer care?

The inevitable knock came sounded from the door and seemed to echo through the entire house. Peeking through the curtains and out the window, she could see Sarah and Hannah standing at the door. Resigning herself to her unavoidable fate, she opened the door to confront her visitors and their nosey questions. She would have preferred to do this when she had better control of her emotions, but she was powerless to pick the time when someone else would visit.

The two ladies were invited in, but before they could even ask a question, Gomer began the conversation. "Well, I guess you can see why I left that man in the first place" Before she could continue, another knock came on the door. "I guess that would be Rachel," she said. When she opened the door, sure enough, Rachel stood waiting to enter. "I was just telling the other girls that the reason I left Hosea was made obvious today."

Although her visitors sat, Gomer could not stay seated. She paced the floor in anger. "How would you like it?" she asked. "How would you like to be married to such a person? I'll be the laughing stock of the temple. No clients will probably want to visit me anymore."

"Gomer, please," Hannah requested, "calm down. It's not good to get so upset."

"It is not as bad as you think," continued Sarah. "Nobody blames you for what happened."

"We know that it wasn't your fault," added Rachel. "no one will think less of you because of this."

"If anything, they will just blame your husband," said Sarah.

"Besides, everybody knows how prophets are," consoled Hannah. "You never know when they are going to…"

"Erupt like a volcano?" offered Gomer in conclusion. The other three women all laughed at this remark. Even though she still wanted to embrace her rage, Gomer found that she couldn't help but smile with them.

"There it is," remarked Sarah, "There is the smile we know and love."

"Anyway," concluded Gomer, "that's just one of the many reasons I left Hosea and his God. I'm much better off serving Baal."

"Don't you ever miss your children, though?" asked Hannah.

"Well, of course I do," she answered. "I'm not completely without feeling, you know. I think about them a lot. I wonder what they are doing or how tall they have gotten. But I can't subject them to be torn between two worlds. It's better I sacrifice seeing them. "

"Well, Hosea will take good care of them, won't he?" asked Sarah.

"Yes He will," Gomer conceded. "Despite all of his glaring, embarrassing faults, he is a good father to the children. I couldn't bear to leave them with someone who would neglect or abuse them. I just feel that they should have a peaceful existence. When our lives are so directly diverse from each other, I think shuffling them back and forth would be too complicated for them."

"Did you see Bianca following him out the gate?" asked Sarah. "

"Yes," answered Gomer, "but I was too upset to think much about it."

"All we know is she followed him out the gate and came back a few minutes later crying her eyes out. She went straight home and no has seen her since," stated Sarah.

"We think she probably threw herself at him. You know she always had a thing for him. And she probably rejected her completely," continued Hannah.

"Maybe she even tried to beg him to take her and when he rejected her, he shamed her to tears," concluded Rachel.

"Well, if your ideas are anywhere near the truth, I wish he had taken her. Then he could forget about me," answered Gomer.

"I can't help but think about poor Bianca," sympathized Hannah, "sitting all alone in her home, crying her poor eyes out. My heart goes out to her."

"Look," replied Gomer, "we don't even know for sure what really happened. Before our bleeding hearts completely bleed out, I think we ought to find out what happened. Don't you?"

The girls all nodded in agreement and started planning how they could approach Bianca and find out what happened. It was decided that they didn't want to all go together or Bianca might feel that she was being pressured and put on the spot. Hannah was the closest to Bianca and so she ought to be the one to visit her.

The next day Hannah went to Bianca's home and rapped on her door. It was a long time before she got an answer. Hannah began to think maybe Bianca wasn't home. Soon, however, Bianca opened the door to her friend and let her in.

"We were wondering what happened to upset you the other day," was Hannah's opening remark. Bianca didn't give an immediate reply. "I hope you know that we care about you," Hannah ventured on, "and was wondering if there was anything we could do to help."

"Help?" Bianca timidly questioned. "No, nobody can help me. I'm beyond pathetic."

"Maybe you would feel better if you told me," said Hannah. "You know that you can tell me anything. I won't judge you or anything like that. We're old friends."

"I don't know if it will help anything, but I may as well tell you." After a long pause she continued. "I asked Hosea to take me, if Gomer wouldn't go with him. He refused. I don't think he was half listening to me. All he could think about was her. So, I pathetically ended up begging to have me on any terms and still he…just brushed my offer aside, like someone would throw out the garbage."

"Oh Bianca, I'm so sorry. Didn't he have any regard for your feelings at all?"

"If he did, he didn't show it. I walked away abased to the very dust and I don't think he even noticed. Oh, I should be laughing. It's really funny. What I desperately wanted, on any terms, Gomer wouldn't even take. I must be the laughing stock of the whole compound."

"No! No you are not. Don't even think that way. Most people don't even know what happened, and besides, those of us who do, love you too much to laugh."

"You know, these prophets of Jehovah are a narrow minded lot. They want their lives to be all one way. They want one God, one law," after a long pause she added, "one woman,"

Hannah walked over and threw her arms around Bianca, who responded in kind. Yet, as Hannah held her friend she couldn't help but feel that something had changed drastically. They stood in close proximity but there was a great gulf fixed between them. A line had been crossed that would separate them for the rest of their lives. Things would never be the way they once were.

Hannah went back to Gomer's place and was surprised to find the others had all gathered there. She wanted to give her report but Rachel had one that was more pertinent.

"Hannah, we're glad you're back," said Gomer with a worried look. "Rachel was just telling us that there are more women missing."

"You mean, besides Esther?" asked Hannah.

"Yes,' answered Rachel. "You know Sharon and Judith? Well, they are gone too."

"You mean they got taken to the slave market?"

"We don't know for sure, but we did see Esther there," answered Gomer. "What else could have happened to them?"

"This whole thing is starting to get on my nerves," said Sarah. "Every time you turn around someone comes up missing. It makes you wonder if they're going to get to us next."

With Hosea coming to visit and causing such a commotion, Gomer had temporarily forgotten about the slave market and how much it had concerned her and her friends. Now, the reality of it had come back to slap them all in the face. None of the women wanted to admit how worried they really were about this situation, but it greatly concerned each one.

"We're a lot younger than those women were," stated Hannah, attempting to encourage everyone else. Even as she spoke it, she knew that the person she was really trying to convince was herself.

"Yes, but we are going to get older someday," replied Sarah. "I for one would like to have an answer. I don't want to be worrying all the time I get older that I will one day be a slave."

"How could we find out?" asked Rachel.

"I think we should go and ask the High Priest," answered Gomer. "I'll bet he could tell us what we want to know."

"Are you sure he will tell us the truth?" asked Sarah.

"Well who else can we ask?" enquired Gomer. "Besides, a High Priest of Baal wouldn't lie to any of Baal's girls. Would he?"

They all concurred that he wouldn't lie to them. At least they hoped that he wouldn't do such a thing. So the agreed that on the next day they would meet and approach the High Priest. They knew that it wouldn't be an easy matter. A person didn't just casually walk up a person of his stature and pepper him with questions. However, they hoped that, if they all came as a group, he would agree to give them an audience.

When they arrived at the temple, the next day, they found out that even making an appointment to see the High Priest was not so simple.

The clerk at the desk wanted to know the purpose of their visit. He wasn't about to let them get away with just saying that their visit was of a personal nature. He demanded that they tell him the nature of their business or he would not allow them an appointment.

"We want to ask him a question," stated Sarah.

"What kind of a question?" the clerk gruffly asked.

"The kind that only the High Priest can answer," retorted Rachel. "If we thought you could answer it, we would ask you."

Now the clerk was adamant. He was about to flat out refuse them any appointment, but, at that moment the High Priest came out of his office door.

"There he is," stated Gomer, "he seems to be free now. Ask him if he can see us."

It was obvious that the High Priest could hear them and also that he was not occupied at the moment. Therefore, he made an effort to appear that he was always willing and even anxious to talk to Baal's girls and put any concerns that they might have to rest.

"Ladies," he said with as much cheerfulness as he could muster. "Won't you come into my office and let me know what I can do for you."

Sarah spoke for the rest of them when she stated. "We have been concerned about the older women of our community who seem to have come up missing."

"Oh, which ones were you referring to?"

"Well, there is Esther, Sharon and Judith."

"Those ladies were sent to the retirement home where they will be taken care of." The four women looked at one another. They all knew that they were not being told the entire truth. No one came out and told him that they had seen Esther being sold as a slave. It seemed that each one realized the wisdom in not telling the man all that they knew. They all consented in silent agreement.

"We thought it was strange that we never got to say goodbye to them," Gomer finally stated.

"Well, it's customary to fill a vacancy at the retirement home as soon as it becomes available. I assure you that they are comfortable and well taken care of. Now, if there is nothing further would you excuse me. I am a very busy man."

"Would it be possible for us to visit them?" asked Hannah.

"You are much too busy in your services here at the temple of Baal. You are all doing a splendid job and your work is very important." Immediately, the clerk entered and the four women were escorted out of the High Priest's office and into the temple.

"Maybe we should have told him about Esther," remarked Sarah as they were leaving the temple.

"No, I think it is better this way," answered Rachel. "This way, we know that he didn't tell us the whole truth, but he doesn't know that we know."

None of the women were sure if their secret knowledge gave them an advantage or not. None of them could imagine how they would defend themselves if their worst nightmare came true. Also, none of them felt any reassurance after their visit to the high priest.

"If this is going to happen, I hope it does within the next fifteen years," stated Sarah.

"Why the next fifteen years?" asked Rachel.

"You know. That's the Jubilee, when all the slaves go free. If it happens later than that, we'll be slaves for life."

They had forgotten about their earlier concern for their friend, Bianca. Gomer had forgotten about her embarrassment over Hosea's visit. Each woman clung tenaciously to the hope that the Jubilee would set them free if they ever became slaves. Little did they know that within six months an even greater fear would seize their hearts. This time it was not the mere fear of slavery but, it was a threat that endangered their very lives.

CHAPTER ELEVEN

Every day for the next six months went by much like the one before. The anxiety caused by the fear of eventually being sold into slavery persisted. The activities of certain days caused them to pay less attention to it, which relieved their concerns to a certain extent. Yet, on another day something would happen or someone would say something that would cause their apprehensions to return.

Gomer no longer had anyone attempting to visit her. It's as if her whole family finally gave up on her. Word had been left at the gate not to allow Hosea to enter, but by the time it was given, it was redundant. He never made an attempt to come in and he was never even seen around the temple area. In a way, this pleased Gomer. She felt relieved that she did not have to argue with relatives and that she wasn't required to explain their visits to her friends. Yet, she wasn't totally happy about the situation. Being forgotten about and ignored wasn't very fulfilling either.

The girls had all learned that their suspicions about Bianca and her attempt to get Hosea to take her instead of Gomer had failed. They suspected that she had practically begged him to take her, and she had. Yet, none of them wanted to exclude Bianca from their circle of friends. They loved her and were willing to continue in friendship as they had before.

Bianca seemed to feel differently about it. When they invited her to go places and do things with them, she responded with reservations. After her self-inflicted humiliation, she was never the same as she had been before. Gone was her quick wit and delightful sense of humor. She rarely smiled these days. When she did join the group, it was usually for short periods of time. She hardly ever shared an opinion and she never initiated a get-together. It's as if she had left with Hosea and this woman who was left in her place, no one knew.

After their unfulfilling visit to the High Priest, the girls noticed that older women were not disappearing quite so rapidly as before. Those that did come up missing were ones that they didn't know and it was hard to be sure the circumstances under which they left. Still, they all kept a sharp eye out to see if anyone was suddenly gone.

Then something happened that made them forget all about slavery and their fear of it. This was something that had never happened there before. It was something that virtually crippled them with fear. A neighboring nation of Israel, the Ammonites were experiencing a drought, and they had come to the Temple of Baal for help.

The people of Ammon were distant relatives of the Israelites. They were the descendants of Lot, their founding father, Abraham's nephew. Lot had an incestuous relationship with his daughter and the child that was born from this was Benammi, the father of the Ammonites.

The Ammonites worshipped the god of fire, Molech. In the worship of Molech, human sacrifices were made. Usually, it was children that was thrown into a big caldron of fire and burned alive. Sometimes an adult, usually a virgin was sacrificed as well. These sacrifices would appease the great god of fire, Molech.

Whenever there was a strange weather pattern or some other unusual phenomenon, the Ammonites thought a sacrifice had to be made, because Molech was displeased. At this time they were experiencing a drought. No rain had fallen in weeks, despite all the sacrifices that were made. Some national official came up with the idea that the Baal worshippers might be able to help. Since the people of Baal believed that their god could control the weather, perhaps one of his girls was sacrificed to their god, Molech, it might bring rain. For a stipulated price, this was agreed upon by the Baal priesthood.

Like a fire in a dry forest, word had spread around the compound that one of Baal's girls was to be chosen to be sacrificed by the Ammonites. All of the women were to gather in certain homes and wait for the guards to come and get the chosen one. Everyone feared that she was the chosen one.

Rachel, Sarah, and Hannah came to Gomer's place. This time they couldn't persuade Bianca to join them. Because of their anxiety, they didn't spend a lot of time trying. The four women gathered in Gomer's living room. No one felt like talking so they all retreated into their own silent world. They listened, intently, fearing that they would hear footsteps approaching their place.

How long they stood in silence, no one remembered. A death like stillness swept over the entire compound. Suddenly they heard them. Footsteps could be heard approaching Gomer's place. The four women automatically began to hold hands and stood wordlessly awaiting someone's fate. Relief swept them when the footsteps could be heard, walking by. They all breathed a sigh of relief, like they had never experienced before.

Strangely enough, no screaming voice of terror could be heard. Somebody must have been chosen, but why had they not cried out? Why was there no begging or pleading? Surely, someone's life was about to end and yet, there was a peaceful silence throughout the whole compound.

Hannah rushed to the window to see if it was possible to learn who the chosen victim was. "Oh no," she cried, putting her hand to her mouth while backing away from the window. The others rushed over to see. They all looked out and seen their friend, Bianca being led silently away. Why wasn't she protesting or fighting? Instead she was being taken without struggle, like a lamb to the slaughter.

Forgetting about their own fears, the four women rushed outside. What were they going to do? They didn't know, but they had to try to do something.

"Can we talk to her?' asked Gomer. "She is our friend."

"You have to ask the priest in charge," the guard curtly answered.

Like a team in motion the foursome moved over to where the priest stood. They were all glad that it wasn't the High Priest. He would probably deny them. "Can we please talk to Bianca before you take her away?"

"What for?" The priest made no attempt to be friendly or courteous.

"She is our friend," one of the girls answered. "And we want to say goodbye," added another. "We know we will never see her again," contributed a third.

"We're in kind of a hurry," the priest protested.

Gomer moved closer to him and said, "Sir, we just want to say goodbye to a friend, surely Baal would not wish for us to be denied that."

With Baal's integrity called into question, the priest relented. "Okay, but be quick about it. We haven't got all day."

They quickly rushed over to Bianca's side and each one took a turn embracing her. Strangely, she didn't look the least bit concerned about her fate. She seemed to be completely accepting it with dignity.

"I'm sorry that you were chosen," said Gomer. "We all are."

"I wasn't chosen. I volunteered."

"But why?" asked Hannah. "Are you that depressed over this business with Hosea?"

"It started out that way, I admit, but then something changed. At first I was so humiliated that I wanted to die. Then I remembered something that Hosea told us. If you remember he said that if we return to Jehovah that He would receive us and heal us. Then he said that Jehovah would love us freely."

"But you're one of Baal's girls. You belong to him," pointed out Sarah.

"Yes, he owns my body but not my soul. I can give that to whatever god I want to."

"We don't know what to say," answered Gomer. "We were all so frightened that it would be us and now you are volunteering. It's almost like you are dying in our place."

"That's what I am doing. I knew that you would be scared and I couldn't let them take you. I can no longer serve Baal. I may belong to him physically, but that is the only way. Don't you see? As long as I am in this body, I can't be divided. I can't serve one god with my body and another with my soul. But if my body and soul are divided, I'm free."

"Are you sure you want to do this?" asked Hannah.

"Positive! I've thought it all through and I'm sure." Bianca paused and then added, "It's funny in a way. Hosea rejected me in one way but in another way he set me free. He spoke the words that I needed to hear. If he had accepted my offer, I might never have thought about his words. And, as for you girls, I love you all and certainly couldn't let this happen to you when I'm at such peace with it."

This is the greatest love I have ever heard of, to die for someone," reasoned Sarah.

"Greater love has no one than this," added Gomer, "to lay down your life for someone else."

Just then, one of the guards grabbed Bianca and began pulling her away. The priest in charge smiled his approval. The girls began to cry. They loaded Bianca on a cart drawn by a mule. Her hands were fettered to the front of the wagon.

Bianca turned to her friends and cried, "When I die, I won't be calling on Baal to save me. I'll do like Hosea said, I'll call on Jehovah. If there is any eternal salvation, I'll hope to find it in Him." She tried to shout something else but the noise of the people taking her away drowned her out. Although they would like to have heard what she said, they knew that they had heard the important part of what she tried to tell them. When she knew that she could no longer be heard, she turned and was transported away. She never again looked back. The girls watched her until their friend was out of sight.

As they turned to walk away, they noticed the High Priest observing the proceedings. In anger, Hannah brazenly rushed up to him and asked, "Is this another person taken to the retirement home?" He typically ignored her and continued speaking to the priests around him.

As they walked away, Hannah remarked to the others, "I hope she didn't do this because she was depressed."

"I don't think she did," answered Gomer. "She seemed to have a purpose in what she was doing. I'm sure that depression didn't cause this."

"According to what she said, Hosea sort of saved her," remarked Rachel. "By refusing her, romantically, he saved her spiritually. Isn't that something?"

"Well, I don't know how true that is," stated Gomer, "but Bianca seemed to believe it."

"She always seemed to have a thing for Hosea," reasoned Hannah. "Maybe on some spiritual level, they somehow connected." Gomer just looked at her as she walked along and said nothing. Her heart ached for her friend. She wished that all this had not happened and they could have pulled Bianca back to the person she used to be. Why couldn't the Ammonites solve their own problem and leave them alone.

One thing this experience ought to teach us," stated Sarah. "Our lives are not worth too much in the world of Baalism." No one tried to dispute her remark. After this terrible day, the scariest of their lives, they all went home.

CHAPTER TWELVE

A period of seven years passed since the day Bianca had been taken away. Strangely enough, during this time, there were few changes in the lives of the four women who witnessed her departure. They had all settled into an almost comfortable, yet guarded existence. They had grown closer and more dependent on each other, with each passing year.

The women spoke often of Bianca and her willing sacrifice. Her memory had taken on legendary proportions in their minds. They cherished her memory the way one does that of a war hero or an ancient explorer that blazed the trails to establish a new country. In their memories, Bianca's faults had vanished away and her virtues were magnified. They were proud that she had been their friend.

The leaders of Baal worship had the foresight to build a retirement home. The older women were taken there and the others were allowed to visit. None of the originals were to be found there. If anyone asked about them, she was told that the person in question had passed on. The priests kept it a secret that the women relocated in the home were later sold as slaves. This method was instituted to keep the questions down and brought peace to all the girls of Baal. However, suspicions about what was truly happening arose and the silent fears were never gone to stay.

During this time, Gomer never received an outside visitor. Her sustenance continued as abundant as ever and she was basically a contented person. Then one day after all these years she got a letter from a doctor, whose name she did not recognize. Upon reading it, she learned that her father, Dibliam had been sick for a long time and was failing fast. The letter asked if she could come and visit. After receiving permission, she went to her father's house for the first time in many years.

The old house looked the same as it always did. Her father was never a person to spend much time redecorating. He liked things to be the way they always were. Gomer smiled as she walked inside and looked around. Some of her own bowls and cups were in the place she had kept them as a young girl. Her bed room had not been slept in since she left home. The living room chair that her mother died while sitting in, had not been moved out of the place it was in on that awful day.

She entered her father's bedroom. He was sleeping and she hated to wake him but needed to do so because her visit was brief. She had a difficult time in her attempts to awaken him. She shook him and called "Daddy," numerous times. He would open his eyes only to have them close again automatically. He would start to stir, but in a few seconds he would be lying still again. Finally, after this process was repeated many times, he was awake to stay. He fixed his eyes upon his daughter and stared silently at her. She moved over to embrace him while he was lying down. His responding hug was very weak. Was he too weak to hug her or was he reluctant to do so because he detested her lifestyle? She couldn't tell for sure.

"I got the doctor's letter," she said in opening the conversation. Still, he was unresponsive. "The doctor said that you were not feeling very well." He attempted to answer but all that came out of his mouth was a rasping sound.

"Let me get you some water," she said and then proceeded to the water jar to pour a drink. When he drank it, he seemed to be able to speak a little better.

"Thanks," was all he managed to get out at first. After another drink and a brief pause, he managed to say, "I'm glad that you came."

"So, how are you really feeling?" she asked.

"Truthfully?"

"Yes," she answered.

"The truth is, I'm dying," he openly admitted. "My earthly journey hasn't got too many more steps to go."

She wanted to deny his statement and tell him not to speak in such a way, but something restrained her. His straightforwardness had disarmed any protest she might have been able to muster.

"I'm glad that you came. There is something…" he began to cough and it was a long time before he could get his breath again. "Could I have some more water?" he asked. Gomer rushed to pour him another cup. He drank part of it and said, "I was trying to say that there is something I must tell you."

"Daddy, if you are going to try to get me to leave the temple and return to Hosea, forget it."

"You know, he has never looked at another woman."

"I'm not surprised. One of my friends offered to go with him the time he came to the temple and he turned her down flat."

"She couldn't have been much of a friend if she offered herself to you husband," Dibliam stated.

Gomer's mind went back to the day when they took Bianca away to her death." That's not true. There was never a better friend. She gave her life so the rest of us wouldn't have to fear death. Oh, she was a little mixed up, sometimes, but she was a good friend."

"After all that's happened, you still remain at the temple of Baal?"

Gomer chose to ignore all the fears the women experienced about being sold as slaves and her pride would only allow her to tell her father about the better parts of their life at the temple. "Of course I want to stay there. They treat us good and we have none of the restrictions that you people who worship Jehovah do."

"I thought by now you might see it differently," he confessed. "And the other girls? Do they feel the same way?"

"Of course they do," she lied. "None of us would ever want to leave.

"I heard that after five years with Baal, you can no longer leave, even if you want to." Dibliam surprised his daughter with his knowledge of the world that she lived in. She looked at him and wondered what else he knew about her life. Did he know about her secret fears? Did he know about the slave sales? She decided to proceed with the conversation as if he didn't and hope it was true.

"Well, none of us would want to leave, even if we could," she boasted. He seemed unfazed about her claim of loyalty to Baal. Did he believe her? She couldn't tell.

"Are you sure that it isn't just your pride talking?" Again, he hit the nail on the head. He seemed to be able to see through her like she was made of glass. How do you defend yourself against someone who knows you so well?

'No," she lied again, "that's how I really feel."

"And how are you doing as far as your living style is concerned? Are you being recompensed well for your services?"

At last he asked her something that she could answer truthfully. Her sustenance had always been plentiful. She didn't know why, but for some reason, she always received more in food supplies and other goods than the other of Baal's girls.

"Yes Father," she stated with confidence. "I have been always provided for. The priests and worshippers must have always been satisfied with my services. I have been supported well." She smiled with confidence. Her libations had always been a source of pride to her. They enabled her to tell herself that she didn't need Hosea. She could make it on her own.

"That's what I wanted to tell you," he said, "I promised Hosea that I wouldn't tell you." He coughs very hard and finds it difficult to catch his breath. After drinking some more water, Gomer fetches the jug and refills his cup. "It is about your support at the temple."

"Yes," she asked, unable to disguise her curiosity. "What about my support?"

"It came from Hosea. It was always from him. He didn't want you to know but he said he didn't want a wife of Jehovah to be supported by worshippers of Baal."

Gomer was shocked. She had never suspected this. It had been her source of pride all these years and now with one sentence, it was all taken from her. "Are you sure?" was all she could think of saying.

"I knew that day I visited you at the temple compound and I wanted to tell you but Hosea made me promise not to. I thought you would find out some other way, but I guess you didn't"

"No, I never knew." Gomer couldn't help but feel anger at being fooled this way. "I don't know as I like the idea of being fooled. Somebody could have told me. Did everybody know but me?"

"I don't think anyone but the High Priest and maybe some of his subordinates. I'm sure none of Baal's girls knew," he stated, hoping to reassure her. "Now, I need to ask you another question about something I heard that happens at the temple."

Gomer wished that she had more time to dwell on her father's last surprising revelation but followed his questioning anyway. "What is it that you have heard?"

"That the older women are sold as slaves after their usefulness as one of Baal's girls is over."

"Do you know everything about my life? I guess some of them have been sold, but they have a retirement home for older women now."

"I heard that they are sold right out of the home. That it is just a cover-up to keep you girls from asking questions."

She didn't want to admit it, but this is what Gomer and her friends had feared for years but wasn't sure. Here was her father, not even living in the compound and seemed to know more about it than she did. Well, there was still one piece of information she could give him that she hoped would relieve his fears as it had assured her.

"We suspected that this might be true but we still have hope of not spending our entire lives in slavery," she said, hoping her words sounded as confident as she pretended to be.

"Yes," he answered, "the Jubilee is in eight years." He leaned over to her, dreading to have to tell the information that she obviously didn't know. "I am sorry to have to tell you this, my daughter, but the Jubilee is for Jehovah worshippers. Baalism has no Jubilee. Once you become a slave under Baal, you are a slave for life."

He might as well have hit her with a brick. Her sense of shock could not be kept from registering on her face. For all these years she kept saying that Baal offered more freedom than Jehovah did and it did, at first. However, as the years roll on, it seems that the opposite was true. Jehovah, through the Jubilee had a means of setting slaves free, Baal did not. The cement was easy to get into when it was wet, but now it was set and she was trapped.

"I tried to tell you this, years ago but I couldn't seem to make you understand."

"I guess you know more about my religion than I do," she quietly replied.

For the rest of the visit, Dibliam tried to tell Gomer about the family. Jezreel had left home to try his hand at farming. He had abandoned his earlier ambitions of being a priest of Baal. Rahumah and Ammi were still at home, helping their father. Rahumah had become quite a little homemaker. Gomer was interested and she tried to listen, but her father's earlier statements had rocked her to the very core of her being.

As Gomer was saying goodbye, she knew that it was the last time she would ever see her father and this filled her with sadness. His final statement was, "Daughter, if there is any way you can ever get out of there, please promise me you will take it."

This time she had no energy to mount a defense about her life. Instead of arguing with him she meekly said, "I promise." On her way back to the compound she thought of how different her life might have been if she hadn't been so angry, prideful and stubborn. She thought of running away from Baal and going back to Hosea, but she knew this was impossible. The priests of Baal had a legal claim on her now that she had served over five years. She decided not to tell the others what she had found out. There was no point is alarming them unnecessarily when none of them could do anything about it.

She walked into a strong, cold wind as she made her way back to the place she called home for many years, but now seemed more like a prison.

CHAPTER THIRTEEN

Hosea watched Rahumah sweeping the floor. She was only twelve years old and yet it seemed like she had been running this household forever. She cooked and cleaned with regularity. It seemed to come natural to her. He couldn't ever remember hearing her complain. He felt bad that she had been thrust into such an adult role in life at such a young age. Her friends at school were allowed to be children throughout their formative ages. Not Rahumah, she was forced to be the woman of the house while she was still very young.

Someday, someone would come calling for the purpose of making Rahumah his wife. A fine wife she would make, too. Yet, Hosea dreaded this day. He tried not to let this happen, but he had come to rely on her for so many things. He just couldn't seem to help himself. He had a large hole in his life that Rahumah had gone a long way towards filling. Not only did she take complete charge of the home but she was company to her father. What would he ever do without her?

Ammi did his part also. He chopped wood and carried it in. He started fires for his sister and even did some repairs on the house. He also did his part without a word of self-pity or dread. The older his children got, the more they took charge of the home. They both knew that their father had been hurt and they had grown up trying to alleviate his pain.

Jezreel was another matter. He was different than the younger ones. He never volunteered to do anything to help around the house. Everything Hosea asked him to do, he did reluctantly. Every move he made seemed to say, "If Mother was still here, I wouldn't have to be doing this. But you drove her away and now everything is wrong." How his heart ached for his oldest son.

Many times Hosea had tried to explain to Jezreel about why his mother had left. Never did he seem to believe him. After a while it felt like he was just making excuses and so he quit trying. When Gomer left, she drove a wedge between the two of them that could never be removed, no matter how hard Hosea had tried. So he began ignoring his son's insolence and rude gestures. Thus, the pattern of their relationship was established and it never changed.

Hosea had an uncle on his mother's side of the family who owned a farm. He had no sons to leave the farm to and his daughters had both married men who owned their own property and had no use for his. So, one day Hosea suggested to his mother that she ask her brother about taking Jezreel in to learn the farming business and to one day inherit the farm. After giving Hosea another of her long lectures about why he needed a real wife and how many ways Gomer had failed to be that wife, she agreed to talk to her brother.

Jezreel jumped at the opportunity. Not only would it get him away from home, where he was forced to live with his failure of a father, but it would give him a start in life. After all, what could the son of a prophet have to look forward to. So, he packed his things and moved to his uncle's house. What he never realized was the hole he had left in his father's home and his heart.

Hosea ached for Jezreel. All the dreams that he had for him when he was born just went up in smoke. He sat in his room for a long time on the day he left. He was too numb to cry. It had been his idea for his son to move out and yet it hurt so badly when he did. Jezreel had been so hard to live with that letting him move to his uncle's place seemed like a perfect solution. Yet, Hosea never expected to feel so empty when the time came for him to move.

First his wife and now his son was gone. Was everyone going to leave him? Was he such a terrible person? Hosea felt like his desires in life were so simple. He never wanted to be successful or famous. He had no desire to be king. All he ever wanted was to please God and have a loving family about him. He always thought that he would be a good husband. He would treat his wife like a queen and his children as they were gifts from God. How had it all gone wrong?

He tried to treat Gomer like a queen at first, but as time had gone on, she never felt like a queen being married to him. He wanted her to so badly, but she didn't. His oldest son had grown to hate him. He loved Jezreel but was totally incapable of making him know that. Being left behind seemed to be his lot in life. Rahumah and Ammi were only twelve and ten years old. He knew that the day would come that they would leave him too. Emotionally, he leaned too hard on his younger children, but he couldn't seem to help himself.

As he sat on his son's bed, he noticed something in the corner of the room. At first he didn't know what it was. He got up and went over to pick it up. It was a little hammer that he had given Jezreel a few years back for his birthday. He was so proud when he gave it to him. It was like saying to his son that soon you'll grow up and use a hammer like a man. Now Jezreel was gone and he didn't even consider the hammer worth taking with him. Hosea held it to his face and couldn't stop the tears.

If Jezreel wanted to hurt his father, he will never know how successful he had been. He had wounded him to the very core of his being. He would put the hammer in a safe place. Maybe Jezreel would remember it and come back for it one day. That day never came. The hammer remained where Hosea had put it on the day of his departure. The pain that it caused never went away.

Hosea's prophetic ministry had gone on as consistent as ever. Occasionally he would feel the spirit of God moving inside him and he knew there would be an occasion coming up for him to give his prophetic message. He had been inspired to tell the people that they had departed from God. This he could do with feeling because his wife had departed from him . He also told them that they didn't really know the Lord and this lack of knowledge was destroying them. The people had backslidden from their God like a young heifer who has a tendency to pull backward when someone is trying to pull her forward with a rope around her neck. This backslidden condition had brought the people into the valley of trouble, yet in that valley God always provided a door of hope that will allow them to return to Him.

Hosea knew that Jehovah would take the people back if they returned to Him. He had faithfully told the people that. The impact of this truth was not lost on Hosea because he would take Gomer back even after she had been gone for all those years. He would love her freely, without bringing up her rebelliousness. He knew that God would love His returning people much more freely than he would Gomer.

He had been faithful in telling the people that they would know the Lord if they would follow Him and this knowledge would enlighten them in all other areas of knowledge as well. Knowledge of God would enrich their whole lives, if the people would only let it.

Yet despite all of his faithfulness in delivering Jehovah's message, Hosea still felt like a failure, in many ways. He was a failure as a husband because he lost his wife. He was a failure as a father because his first begotten son had left him. He even felt like a failure as a prophet. He had failed to get his message across to very many people. His faithfulness did not make him a success.

There were some prophets that the people referred to as Major Prophets, like Isaiah and Jeremiah in the south. These prophets had declared their message before kings and they had lengthy messages, which contained many insights about the coming Messiah. Hosea's messages were short and to the point. He had no lengthy messages and he never had a king in his audience nor did he ever speak in the king's court. There was no way around it, Hosea was the least among the minor prophets.

Hosea's mother had never lost her willingness to tell him that he could have done better at picking out a wife and how foolish he was for not taking on another wife. Usually, after a meeting with her lady friends, she would be filled with new enthusiasm to straighten her son out. Hosea's failed marriage always provided the ladies with fodder for their gossip. Anyone would think that after seven years, the subject would die out. That never happened. These ladies seemed to come up with some new angle that relit the fire of their conversation. This always gave Mother a new approach to make to her foolish son.

Hosea could never understand their supposed interest in his family life. Like a ship that sank to the bottom of the ocean, no amount of words could ever bring it back up and set it to sailing again. Yet these ladies talked on and on. Also, Mother's corrections went on and on as well. Hosea's ears, already calloused to the subject, grew more and more insensitive.

Amos had always been a faithful friend. He never chided or corrected Hosea. If anyone understood that Hosea's faithfulness to his wife was also faithfulness to God, it was him. He visited a lot in the early days of Hosea's loneliness. However, his own prophetic ministry kept him quite busy. Although Amos was never a very popular prophet, he, at least spoke his message in the king's court from time to time. Hosea was never to know what that was like.

So, here he sat, alone in his room. If not for his two youngest children, he would feel like he had wasted his life. Regardless of this small victory, Hosea considered himself to be a failed man. He failed in marriage as well as failing as a father to Jezreel. He never wanted to fail those people. He wanted to meet all of their needs, but he couldn't seem to do so.

The success of his prophetic ministry could be questioned as well. Who had he touched with his ministry? Who had he helped? Even though he was never very successful in ministry, he would be as faithful to it as he could. This he intended to do for the rest of his life.

CHAPTER FOURTEEN

As Gomer entered the temple grounds, she detected an aura of difference that she couldn't understand. Two younger women walked passed her. They ignored her as they chattered and continued walking. She had been too amazed by their presence to attempt a greeting. They probably wouldn't have answered her anyway. She didn't know all of Baal's girls, personally, but she recognized each one. Those two young ones were new to her.

Before she got to her home, two more girls who were completely unfamiliar to her passed her by. This time she did attempt to greet them. They exchanged her greeting so quickly and so insensitively that she couldn't question them as to when they arrived. Over across the huge lawn, she saw other girls. They were all new and they were all young.

When she arrived to her home, she saw Rachel and Sarah, sitting on her porch. They arose to greet her with concerned expressions on their face. "Gomer, where have you been?" asked Sarah. "We need to talk to you."

"I've been to see my sick father?" she quickly answered. "Who are all these new girls and when did they get here?"

"That's what we need to talk to you about." answered Rachel. "Hannah is gone!"

"Gone? What do you mean gone? Where is she gone to?" Neither of her friends answered. Their silence made the answer obvious. "Oh no," Gomer fairly groaned. "It can't be. She was younger than me."

"I know," said Sarah, "she was the youngest one of us."

"That isn't all," said Rachel. "We heard that all of the women like us. You know, the ones who have been here a while are going to be shipped out."

"To where?" asked Gomer. She already knew the answer but she was hoping beyond hope that they could tell her something different.

"To the slave sale," whispered Sarah.

"What about the retirement home?" asked Gomer.

"We knew that was just a ruse." answered Sarah. "Everybody knew."

"That's why they have to get rid of us," added Rachel.

"And they felt that if they had newer, younger girls for Baal that they would attract more people in the temple."

"Are you sure that this is true?" asked Gomer.

"We tried to ask one of the priests and he just laughed at first," said Rachel.

"Then we told him the rumor we heard and he told us not to believe everything we hear," added Sarah.

"What about the High Priest? Did you ask him?"

"Ha, that's a joke," answered Sarah. "He is gone for the day, maybe for the week. He probably didn't want anyone asking questions."

"What can we do?" asked Gomer.

Sarah sighed and answered, "There is nothing to do but sit and wait for them to come and get us."

"And hope that they don't," added Rachel.

"When did they take Hannah away?" asked Gomer.

"She wasn't here this morning so they must have come in the middle of the night," said Rachel. "There were a few others taken too."

"Well, I think that the best thing we can do is to go about our business as if nothing happened," counseled Gomer. "Maybe the quota of slaves will be filled and they will leave us here." All the girls knew that what Gomer said wasn't likely to happen but it gave them a sliver of hope to hang on to.

With uneasy hearts the three women separated and went home. None of them slept well that night. When they awoke in the morning and went out and about, they discovered that no one else was missing. The same thing happened for the next two days, causing their small hopes to grow and take on strength.

By the third day, their nerves were more settled and they found it within themselves to laugh and joke. Not like they did before, but a few attempts at gaiety were made which helped calm their nerves a little. Maybe the rumors were wrong and they were never intending to take everybody, just the few that were already missing. They were sorry that Hannah was taken, but they were glad that the three of them were still together.

On the fourth morning, terror struck again. Other women were missing. Rachel met Gomer at the well with the frightful news. "Gomer, I think others are missing. Those two women who live down the lane have not been seen. There are others too."

"What about Sarah?" asked Gomer, unable to mask the fear that she felt. "Have you seen her?"

"No, I just found out about the others on my way over here. Let's go and see if we can find her." The two of them proceeded toward Sarah's house. They walked silently, each one locked in their own terrifying world. Just as they walked up to the house, Sarah was starting out the door. The moment she laid eyes on her friends, she knew that something was wrong.

"What are you two doing here?" she asked.

"More women are missing and we were coming to check on you," replied Gomer.

"And you thought maybe I was…" The sentence was too horrible to complete, but they all knew what the ending was.

"I'm not sure that I like this idea of sitting around and waiting," stated Rachel.

"But, what else can we do," asked Gomer. "Do you have a better idea?

"Yes, I'm going to go and tell them that if they are going to sell me anyway, to do it today and get it over with."

"Oh, Rachel," moaned Gomer, "you don't want to do that. Maybe they won't get to you and you will escape. But if you turn yourself in, you'll be a slave for sure."

"But I just can't stand this waiting around," she nervously answered. "Besides, the Jubilee is in a few years and I will be set free."

At this point, Gomer made a decision to tell her friends what she learned at her father's house. "Listen, I've got something to tell you. I just found out the other day and I was going to spare you this, but since we are all in this together and being sold is even more of a threat, I feel I have to tell you."

"What is it?" asked Rachel.

"The Baal people have no Jubilee. That's only for followers of Jehovah, not Baal. If we are sold as slaves now, we are slaves for life." Her two friends were shocked. Neither of them seemed to know what to say. "I was surprised too. I guess, in the long run, Jehovah offers more freedom than we thought."

The next morning, Rachel was gone. Did she turn herself in or did they take her? Gomer and Sarah could not be sure. Did she call for them as she was being led away and they were too asleep to hear her screams?

The two temporary survivors commiserated all day. They both chided themselves for not hearing their friend being taken away. But even if they did, what could they have done?

The next night, Gomer was unable to fall asleep. What if they came for her? Sure enough, at about three o'clock in the morning she heard footsteps coming down the road. She lay still hoping that they would pass by her house, but it seemed that her worst nightmare was coming true. They started to turn in to her house. She sprang from her bed and rushed out the back door. Instinctively, she headed for Sarah's house. Maybe Sarah could hide her or something.

Gomer got as far as her friend's driveway when the guards seized her from behind. "Sarah, Sarah," she called, but the house remained dark and still. Had Sarah already been taken or was she sleeping too soundly to hear her. Over and over she called while she was fighting her captors. The dark house refused to answer. She knew that Sarah couldn't do anything now anyway, but she hoped that she could let her know what was happening to her.

In a moment, Gomer had freed herself from the grasp of her captors. Immediately she started to run, but where could she go? Nowhere, but she ran anyway. Like a frightened animal that had been tracked down by hunters, she wildly ran. All pride and dignity had been stripped away from her and she was completely in a survivor mode.

Gomer heard her pursuers behind her. They didn't seem angry or upset that she broke loose. Instead she heard laughter. Why were they laughing? What was so funny about this? Then she realized that they were making a sport out of chasing her. "You grab her," shouted one. Another shouted back, "No, you take her. She's too wild for me."

Gomer thought of the dignity with which her friend, Bianca had faced her fate on that long ago day. It seemed to Gomer that Bianca was the better woman. Hosea would have been better off with her. Here she was, being toyed with by men who were only trying to amuse themselves and were degrading her in the process. Why couldn't she stop herself from screaming? Every time she screamed, she felt like she had abased herself more, but she just couldn't stop.

They had encircled her now. It was impossible to escape. Yet, she could not stop herself from trying. Every attempt she made just stripped a little more of her pride away. Finally, she slumped to the ground in exhaustion. Her body as well as her pride had been utterly depleted. As she was being led away, she hoped that her friend, Sarah had not seen her behaving in such a loathsome manner. She hated herself at that moment. They had reduced her to a trapped animal. Now she was being led away, as if to the slaughter.

Nobody even spoke to her as they led her along. She had been reduced to the lowest creature on the planet and they were merely treating her as such. What's worse, she began to think of herself in the same way. She looked straight ahead as they took her into the temple and out the back. Ordinarily, she would have wanted one last look at a place where she had lived so long. Yet, she was afraid that if she did look back, she would meet the eyes of someone who had seen her humiliating performance.

So this is what being a servant of Baal had got her. This is the way he treats his girls in the end. People had tried to tell her, but she wouldn't listen. She thought that she knew better than they did. She had found out the truth a little too late. Now the future looked so dark and hopeless.

She felt a shiver as she plodded along. Her hands were not free to adjust her disheveled clothing or her messy hair. That was indicative of her life now, no freedom to do anything. All hope was gone. She was glad that Hosea could not see her now. She would be too ashamed to face him. Life as she had once known it was over and all that remained was a living death.

CHAPTER FIFTEEN

"Go, show your love to your wife, even though she is still an adulteress. Love her as the Lord loves the people, even though they turn to other gods." The voice of Jehovah had awakened Hosea from his sleep early in the morning. The voice was unmistakable, he had heard it before. It always brought a thrill to his heart that Jehovah, the creator of the universe would speak to him. It was the first time after all these years that God had even spoke of Gomer.

Even though the hour was early, Hosea sprang from his bed in enthusiasm. Maybe this meant that his marriage would be restored, that Gomer was coming back. For the first time in many years he had a reason to hope. His whole being was alive with expectation.

Then he remembered something. How could he show her his love when he couldn't get past the temple gate? Even if he did somehow get in, would Gomer even see him? All of a sudden, the path to get to his wife to show her his love seemed impossibly blocked.

"Jehovah, how can I see her if they won't let me in?" No answer. "How can I show her my love, if she won't see me?" Again, no answer. Jehovah seemed to be consistent in giving out proclamations without any further comment. Hosea sighed and then he asked no more questions. So, he decided to dwell on God's original and really, his only statement and allow the thrill of it to fill his heart again.

The first word that Jehovah had told him was, "go." So, he decided that this must mean that she wasn't going to come to him, but he must go to her. He decided that he would give this a try. He would go to the temple and see if he could somehow get in.

When he got there he noticed that they had guards at the gate now. They probably instituted this after his last visit. The guard was young. Maybe he could be easily manipulated.

"I would like to enter to see someone," he announced, trying to display a show of confidence.

"Who do you want to see?"

"Gomer."

"Gomer? There isn't anyone here by that name," was the guard's terse response.

"What do you mean? She has been here for years."

"Well, I have a list of Baal's girls," he replied, pointing to the wall where certain notices were posted, "and I'm telling you that we haven't got anyone by that name."

"That's impossible," declared Hosea, "check the list again. I know she is here."

"Wait a minute," stated the guard, with renewed insight, "Didn't you say that she had been here for years?"

"Yes, she has."

"Well that explains it. All of Baal's girls who have served here over five years have recently been retired."

"Retired? What do you mean?"

"All I know is a bunch of older women got retired, just recently. I can't help you and, as you can see I'm kind of busy. So, could you move along?"

"Well, where would they take retired people?"

"I don't know. Do I look like I work for the census bureau?" The guard's patience was obviously wearing thin. "There used to be some sort of a retirement home out back of the compound, you can try there."

"Okay, I will. Thanks," Hosea answered as he started away. He only got two or three steps when he heard the guard call out to him.

"Wait a minute pal. I suddenly realized who you are. I couldn't let you in if that Gomer was still here. You're that idiot that embarrassed everyone with your ranting and ravings some years back. That's you, isn't it?"

"Yeah, that's me," deadpanned Hosea. "I'm that idiot. Now, if you'll excuse me," he added as he hurried along.

When Hosea got to the retirement home, he wasn't sure he had the right place. There was no sign to identify the place as a retirement home. He had asked a number of people and had narrowed it down the best he could and here he was. He had to knock several times before getting an answer. A frail looking, elderly woman answered the door. "Can I help you?" she muttered. She was the picture of nervousness. She was trembling very badly, while gripping the doorpost to support her quivering frame.

"Is there a woman named Gomer living here?" he asked. The question seemed to make her shutter even more than she already was.

"No," she fairly shouted. "No there is no one by that name living here."

"Well, had she been living here? I heard she recently retired."

"She don't live here and I can't tell you nothing more," she whined as she started to close the door.

"Why? Why can't you tell me anything more?" he tried to ask, but she had already closed the door. He could hear her thundering up the stairs inside. It amazed him that such a frail person could make so much noise on the stairs.

He couldn't dwell on this ghost of a woman and why she was so nervous. He had to find Gomer, but how to do so, he couldn't imagine. He tried knocking on the retirement home door again. The answer coming from the house was complete silence. "Lady, please, can't you tell me anything?" he yelled at the locked door. Again, no answer came from inside the house. He could see that this was getting him nowhere, so he left.

Not knowing what else to do, he tried walking the streets to see if he might spot her somewhere, anywhere. This, however, proved to be as unfruitful as his other attempts had been. He had started out with such enthusiasm and now, here he had become a complete failure. Discouraged and confused, he decided to head for home.

On his way home, he decided to go by his friend, Amos' house. Maybe he could shed some light on Hosea's problem. Maybe he would know why Jehovah had told him to do something that was impossible for him to do. First, he was afraid that they wouldn't let him see her and now he can't even find her. Things had gone from bad to worse and now he couldn't help himself. By now he was fearing the worst. He may never see her again.

He found Amos working in his garden. Immediately, Amos knew that something was troubling his friend. Hosea had seldom been upbeat in the last few years, but today he looked lower than usual.

"What's wrong, Hosea?' asked Amos. "You look terrible." At first Hosea just stood in place without talking. His emotions had obviously gotten the better of him. "Why don't we go up to the house," asked Amos, "we can speak there more comfortably."

They both took seats on Amos' porch and then Hosea found his voice. He told his friend about Jehovah's message. Then he continued to tell about his attempt to obey the message and his encounter with the stubborn guard and the fragile woman and her strange behavior. He concluded by telling of the street walking that eventually led him to Amos' place.

Amos responded by telling Hosea, "This is good news, really. Don't you see? It must mean that you will soon be getting her back."

"That's what I thought, at first, but I don't see how. I can't even find her. How can I show her my love?"

"I don't know the details any better than you do, but I know it's going to happen," said Amos confidently.

"How can you be sure?"

"Because Jehovah said so," assured Amos. "He wouldn't tell you to do something if He wasn't going to make the way for it to happen. I know. I've heard God's voice many times and He has never failed.

"It is just that I've waited so long," bemoaned Hosea, "and when I finally get something to hope for, it seems that I have to wait even longer."

"Yes, but, don't you see? Just wait a little longer and see what Jehovah can do." Putting his hand on Hosea's shoulder he added, "Don't give up now. You are on the verge of a miracle."

"Do you think so?"

"Oh I know so," replied Amos. "You have been faithful, Hosea. I know it has been hard and you have gotten discouraged at times, but you are the most faithful person that I know of."

"Oh, I feel like I am anything but that," confessed Hosea.

"Nobody else would have borne the burden that you have. I know Jehovah is about to reward you. This is based on everything that I know about Jehovah and all that I've seen Him do."

"Thank you, Amos. You don't know how much you have lifted my spirits." Hosea's whole demeanor has changed after talking to his fellow prophet.

Now, my friend, you better be getting on home. You've got some house work to do."

"Housework?" questioned Hosea.

"Yes. You've got to be getting things ready and making room. The lady of the house will soon be coming home." Nothing more needed to be said. The two prophets bid each other goodbye and Hosea headed home with lifted spirits and faith in the future.

CHAPTER SIXTEEN

Gomer couldn't remember how long she had been walking. They were taking her to a place totally unfamiliar to her and they were making her walk all the way. Dawn was beginning to breakout over the horizon when they reached a strange building. It looked like some sort of a jail. When they went inside, she was convinced that it was a jail. They locked her in a solitary cell. She could hear them walking out, shutting the heavy door and then everything was silent.

She sat on the edge of the bed and wondered what would happen to her. The women in the other cells were still sleeping. Who were they? What would they be like? Would she find Hannah, Rachel or maybe even Sarah among them? A million questions seemed to plague her mind, all at once. The biggest and most troublesome question was, who would buy her? What would that person be like?

There was no point in denying it any longer. Her way of life had failed. It seemed right in her own eyes to begin with, and she certainly defended it to the hilt. Now there was no one to defend it to. Couldn't even defend it to herself. She had been so cocky, so proud. This pride had come before her fall. It had brought her down to the very dust. It was kind of hard to be sitting in a jail on a cot and was about to be sold as a slave and say she had been right.

What would it have been like if she had stayed with Hosea? She would have been domineered by him and his God, but she would have been spared some dignity. Regret began to eat away at her spirit. Now, she began to wish she had listened to him. She wished she had been more understanding and not so pig headed. That was all water over the dam, now. There was nothing to do but face her bitter fate. Everything seemed that it would be bitter from now on.

With an exhausted body, a troubled spirit and an overwhelmed mind she lay down and was consumed by a fitful, restless sleep. Her dreams didn't make any sense. They were a confused muddle of strange people and disconnected events. Finally, sleep mercifully released her and she woke up. Still she felt totally consumed.

At breakfast, nobody talked. Everyone was lost in their own thoughts, dreading an unfriendly future. She looked around to try to find a familiar face, but found none. Where were her friends? What had happened to them? How she ached for familiarity and thirsted for friendship. She was denied both. Suddenly she realized that the food she was eating was hardly eatable. Did it really taste this bad or were her taste buds as numb as the rest of her being? She never attempted another bite.

Strangely, she was glad to be back in her cell. It was the only hint of familiarity she experienced. Still, she sat there with nothing to do or to occupy herself with. The noon meal was the same. Terrible food served to silent zombies and then they were marched back to the cells.

About the second day of this, Gomer decided to try something different. It would probably be unsuccessful, but what did she have to lose? She had hit rock bottom and could go no lower. Who ever heard of a person sinking lower than rock bottom?

They were all marched to their places at the table and sat there trying to stomach something that could barely be called food. Gomer stood in her place and asked, "Has anyone here seen a girl named Hannah?" The zombies remained in their catatonic state. "That's Hannah, has anyone seen or heard of her?" Again, there was no answer. This wasn't going to be so easy.

"How about Rachel?" she continued to press for information. "Has anyone seen or heard of a woman named Rachel?" None of the women responded.

"Shut up and sit down!" an unidentified voice came from behind her. Then a burly guard carrying a large stick of some sort emerged out of the crowd. "I said, sit down," he ordered.

"Why, is it against the rules to talk here?" she asked. The guard started toward her with a menacing look on his face. Intimidated, she sat down. He stood and stared at her for a long time and then returned to where he had been. Gomer remained silent for the rest of the meal.

On the way back to her cell a small, jittery woman came up behind her and said, "Rachel is in the cells on the other side of the building." Then she scooted past Gomer and hurried on her way. She moved so quickly that Gomer couldn't even form a question to ask her. She probably wouldn't have answered anyway. She would have liked to have asked about Rachel's welfare, but it was now too late.

Gomer decided that at the next meal, she would sit across from the jittery woman and she did. "How do you know where Rachel is?" she whispered to her.

"I was over there where she is until they moved me here. I don't know why they moved me." Just then, one of the guards passed by their table so they suspended conversation until he was out of hearing range.

"Is there any way I can see her?" she asked. The woman remained silent and thoughtful for a few minutes.

"Why do you want to see her? She can't help you. Nobody here can help anyone else."

"I know. I just would like to see how she is doing. She is a friend of mine."

"She was a friend," the lady corrected. "There are no friends here. Whatever you were in the past, you are not anymore."

"What do you mean by that?"

"If they see two people becoming friends they get separated fast and they punish you for it." Another guard sauntered past and they had to quit whispering. He seemed to take forever to pass. He was in no hurry, so he took a couple of steps and stood in place for a while and then took a few more steps. Finally, he passed out of range.

"Punish you? How?"

"Solitary, they lock you up there. They make your life so miserable that you eventually look forward to being sold as a slave to get out of here. Look, we don't have any future so you had better forget the past and this Rachel person."

"I would really like to see her. Is there any way I can?"

"Well I can't promise you anything but there is one guard that isn't as miserable as the others. If I can, I'll ask her, but like I said, no promises."

"That's all I can ask for. Thank you."

Nothing more was said. They returned to their cells and continued their empty, meaningless existence. Gomer waited and waited for something that she wasn't sure was even going to happen. Yet, there was nothing else to do but wait. Eventually she lay down on her bed and dozed off.

Soon she was awakened to the sound of a familiar voice. It seemed to be calling her name. Was she dreaming? At first, she wasn't sure. Then she was awakened and still she heard the voice. "Gomer," she said. Looking up she saw the familiar face of Rachel. It was familiar and yet it looked different, so much older.

"Rachel, I'm glad you came."

"I can't stay long and if I get caught, I will be sent away, but I wanted to see you to tell you…"

"Tell me what?"

"We were betrayed," answered Rachel. "A lot of women in here were betrayed."

"Betrayed, by whom? Who would betray us and why?"

"If you think about it, all of Baal's girls belonged to one clique or another. It was the only form of fellowship that we could have. Ours was with Hannah, Sarah and Bianca."

"Okay, so, what does it mean?"

"One woman out of every group betrayed the others in exchange for a promise that they would never be sold as slaves." She stopped to let this information sink in, but Gomer still didn't get it. Therefore, Rachel continued, "Now think, who in our group never got taken away by the guards?"

Gomer was still having difficulty processing everything that Rachel was saying, but the answer to her question was obvious. "Well, that would be Sarah."

"Exactly!"

"I don't get it. How could she betray us? What did she do?"

"When she found out about the deal, she went to the guards and told them where we lived and answered questions about us. I don't know all about it but she knew that we would be taken and when. She didn't answer when you called to her, did she?" Gomer merely shook her head. "She didn't for me either."

"How do you know this, Rachel?"

"The same guard who let me come here told us all about it."

"You said that you could be taken away. Where do they take you," asked Gomer.

"To the place where they take the incorrigible women, at least that's what they call them. It's some farm or mines or something, I don't know. You're sold cheap and worked to death. Most people die after a couple of years there."

"Oh Rachel, you risked that to come here?"

"You know what, I don't care. I do not care," she repeated, emphasizing each syllable. "If I go there and die, I'll die with the name Jehovah on my lips. Not Baal. Look what serving him got us. I think your husband was right all along. He said Jehovah will forgive us and love us. Well, that's what I want. I'll never pray to Baal again." Rachel stepped back and lifted her voice to shout, "Do you hear that, everybody, I'll never pray to Baal again. I'll pray to Jehovah, never to Baal."

She reminded Gomer of Bianca and the vow she had made so many years before, declaring to pray to Jehovah on her dying day and rejecting Baal.

Before Rachel could utter another sentence, some guards hurried up and grabbed her. As they dragged her away, she kept shouting her promise to pray to Jehovah and her denouncement of Baal. Finally, she could be heard no more.

"Oh, Rachel," Gomer moaned. She stood there thinking of how she just witnessed her friend throwing her life away. She might have made it back to her cell undetected. Why did she do it? Had life here become so terrible that she chose hardship and death over it? On the other hand, Rachel had nothing much to look forward to in life, just suffering, hardship and misery. Maybe her choice wasn't so hard to understand after all.

Then Gomer began blaming herself. She should have left Rachel alone and she would be safely in her own cell. It was her fault that Rachel did what she did. Their lives together had started out so well. They had so much fun together. How had it reached such a bitter conclusion?

The voice of Rachel's tirade would be heard outside Gomer's window. Still she was ranting about her decision to cry out to Jehovah and to refutation of Baal. Gomer rushed to the window to see her friend being led away to wherever they were taking her. The group passed by some worshippers headed for Baal's Temple. "Don't go in there," Rachel yelled. "Worship Jehovah, not Baal, see what serving Baal brought me to." The guards smote Rachel in an attempt to quiet her down. "Go see a man named Hosea, he can help you…" with that having been said they final gagged Rachel and led her out of sight. Strangely enough, some of the people turned and went another way. They didn't go to the temple at all. Maybe Rachel had done some good.

Gomer returned to the privacy of her own thoughts. She began to think of how Sarah had gone behind their backs and betrayed them. She had been talking and laughing with them, knowing all along that she had turned them in. Anger began to well up inside of her. Her own friend had lifted her voice against her. How could such a sweet smiling, soft voiced person do such a thing? Fear for one's own safety can cause even the nicest person to do dastardly things.

Gomer was alone now. Bianca had been long dead. Hannah was obviously sold as a slave. To whom, she did not know. Rachel had just been taken away to face the cruelest of fates. Sarah had betrayed them to save her own skin. Now, Gomer was friendless and facing the unknown. She was powerless to do anything about her destiny. There was nothing to do but wait for it.

CHAPTER SEVENTEEN

Gomer couldn't remember how long she stayed in the temporary holding center after Rachel was taken away. Life there returned to the way it had been before. Nobody talked or interacted in any way. Gomer never again made any attempt to communicate with the others. She had lived among the zombies so long that she had become one of them.

She never again saw the little old lady that told her about Rachel. When Gomer went down to the next meal, she wasn't there. Was she taken away with Rachel? Gomer hadn't seen her with the group when it was leaving. Maybe she died or was sold about that time. Gomer wondered about her, but she didn't care enough to ask.

Three primary emotions flooded Gomer's heart during these days. The first was regret. She could have so easily avoided the fate that she now faced. If only she hadn't been so stubborn and so quick to justify her actions. Yet, there was nothing that she could do about it now. Her second emotion was anger. She inwardly raged that such a trusted friend as Sarah could have done such a dastardly thing as to betray her and Rachel. Maybe even Hannah had been victimized by Sarah's scheme. Her final emotion was guilt. If she had not asked about Rachel, she might have wound up with a better life than the one she obviously face today. It certainly was not her intention to bring such cruelty on Rachel. Her guilt over Rachel sort of modified her anger over Sarah. Who knows, maybe what Sarah had done, she did unwittingly?

Finally, one day the guards came and took some of the women away. Gomer was among them. They were taken to another building to be kept for the slave sale which was to be held the next day. Here they were allowed to bathe and was given cleaner clothes to wear. The food here was much better than it was at the other place. Maybe they were trying to fatten them up in one day. If it wasn't for the pending events of the next day, life here would be tolerable.

On the day of the sale, they were given a strange garment to wear. The middle of it fit over the head and it hung down the front and the back. There was no belt or ties to fasten it on the sides. There were no undergarments for them to wear, so with one sweep of someone's hand they could be totally exposed in no time at all. There was no point in complaining about the garment because the easy removability seemed to be the point in making them wear it.

As she stood at the back, waiting to be taken up to be sold, she counted about a dozen women standing with her. One after another was pulled to the front of the stage and the bidding commenced. Finally it became Gomer's turn. She stood with head bowed feeling such shame as she had never felt before. The inevitable tears wouldn't stop flowing. Her pride had been taken away when they took her clothes. Her dignity dissolved sometime after they took her from her home. Her shame had found an unprecedented depth that she had not previously anticipated.

At first no one even offered a bid. Was she that worthless? The auctioneer began to plead with the bidders that surely someone must see the value of such a prime piece of property as her. She wasn't that old and must have many more years of good hard work left in her. It was shameful enough to be forced into slavery, but now it seemed that no one even wanted her for that. How low could a human being sink? How much degradation could a person take? They no longer wanted her as one of Baal's girls and now it seemed that no one wanted her as a slave.

When it seemed that her humiliation had been piled upon itself, and she was about as naked emotionally as she was physically, she suddenly heard a voice. Someone seemed to be actually bidding for her. Could it be true? Did someone think that she had at least a little bit of worth? There was no mistaking it, someone was actually bidding for her and they seemed to be willing to pay the full asking price for a female slave. Wait a minute, that voice, she had heard it before. It was someone who was familiar and they were buying her. This caused her even more shame. She wanted so very badly to know who it was, but she was too ashamed to lift her head to see who was paying the price for her.

Hosea spent much of the day at home. Jehovah had said nothing more about him returning to his wife and he had no idea how to fulfill the command so he did nothing about it. Jehovah said nothing and Hosea did nothing. He and Jehovah seemed to be at a stalemate. Jehovah wouldn't tell him what to do and he didn't know what to do. He clung tenaciously to the hopeful promise that his friend, Amos had given him. So far, however, nothing had happened to prove him right.

As Hosea rested on his front porch he noticed a couple of his neighbors walking by his house. "Hosea," one of them called, "why don't you come with us?"

"Where are you going?" he asked.

"To the slave sale."

"Oh, I don't know. I don't often go to those places." "Come on," they persisted. "It will do you good to get away from the house."

"Okay, wait up," he answered. Even as he agreed to go, Hosea wondered why he was doing it. Usually, it was unthinkable to go to a place where they sold human beings. The idea of doing so went against everything that he believed in, and yet, this time, it seemed so right to do so. Why he felt like this, he couldn't imagine. So, he found himself leaving his chair and going with his neighbors.

"Don't bring too much money," one of them joked, "you might be tempted to buy someone." They had a good laugh over this and Hosea found himself laughing with them.

"There's not much danger of that happening," he avowed.

When they got to the sale, Hosea saw nothing unusual. He began to feel that he shouldn't have come. Human trafficking certainly did not interest him. He even believed it was morally wrong. Yet, here he stood with all the bidders and buyers. Why he was there, he didn't know. Well, it would be very rude to just walk away so he stayed, prepared to endure it until the end. As he looked around, everyone else seemed to be enjoying themselves. With great enthusiasm, they shouted, whistled and cheered as the poor victims were paraded before the perspective buyers. Hosea began to loath himself and he hoped nobody that he knew would see him there.

Suddenly, he saw her. She was standing in the back awaiting the misery that faced her. He began to move closer to make sure that his eyes were not playing tricks on him.

"Oh, I see he is interested after all," someone joked. Hosea heard laughter behind him but he never stopped because of it. Closer and closer to the front he fought his way, until he stood in the very front. It was her. It was his Gomer, the love of his life being reduced to a slave. He knew that he couldn't let this happen.

He began to move to the back. In a moments time he was changed from a bored bystander to a man with a mission.

"Hey, where are you going? I thought you were against slavery?" one of the men asked in an accusing tone of voice.

"I've seen her," he answered. "I've seen Gomer, my wife."

"Your wife?" one of them asked. "I thought you didn't have a wife."

"He did have a wife," the other countered. "She left him a long time ago. Get this," the speaker placed his hand on the other's shoulder, "she left him to be one of Baal's girls."

"She did?"

"Yup, shamed him right out." Then calling to Hosea he asked, "So where are you going anyway?"

"Home to get my money to buy her."

"Buy her? You're crazy! What do you want to buy her for?"

"Because I love her," with that answer Hosea hurried on home to get his money.

"She ain't worth it," the neighbor kept calling toward Hosea but he kept hurrying away and didn't look back. "She deserves to be a slave. She only brought you shame. You're a fool, Hosea, a fool." The man kept yelling until Hosea was out of hearing range.

Nothing could stop him now. Hosea had a purpose and he meant to fulfill it. He was going to fulfill Jehovah's command and show his love to his wife again. He only hoped that he wasn't too late. He got his money and loaded ten bushels of barley on a wagon and started back to the sale. Then he remembered that there was something else that he needed to get. He went back in and got a robe that she could wear if he could bring her home.

Could this be the fulfillment of Jehovah's command for him to love her again? He hoped so but he didn't have much time to dwell on the thought because he had to hurry. The thought of her being sold before he could get back to her was to threatening for him to dwell on. He had suffered so much heart break over the past few years. If someone else bought her before he got there, the pain would be too much for him to bear. Dismissing all opposing thoughts out of his mind, he hurried on his way.

As he arrived back at the slave sale, he could see Gomer, with head bowed, standing before the crowd. Strangely, the whole place seemed silent. For some reason, nobody was offering a bid for her. He could see the beleaguered auctioneer, trying desperately to coax, even the smallest bid from the people. No voice was raised. No hand was lifted. It was a as if the crowd was collectively saying, "She is worthless. Nobody wants her."

"I'll bid fifteen pieces of silver and ten bushels of barley," Hosea cried out. His voice seemed to pierce the heavy night air like a javelin. All heads turned to see who the bidder was. Everyone was aghast. Even the auctioneer was shocked into momentary silence. Nobody moved or spoke for a few seconds.

"Why, that fool is paying the full price for that worthless scumbag," an anonymous voice cried out. Others began to speak out in agreement.

His neighbors came up beside him and one of them said, "You're so stupid, Hosea. You could have gotten her a lot cheaper than that. Why did you bid so high?"

"She is not worth what you are bidding. She's not worth anything," the other neighbor added.

"I'll pay no less that the full price for her. She is worth it to me," Hosea stubbornly insisted.

"All she ever did was to bring you shame. She shamed your children and tore your home apart. You're stupid to bid anything at all for her," the first one pointed out,

"Haven't you ever loved anyone that much? I mean, so much that you would do anything for her?" asked Hosea.

"No, not that much. If any woman ever did for me what she did to you, I'd kill her. I certainly wouldn't buy her. You're a fool, Hosea. That's all I can say for you."

"Sold to the gentleman in the back for fifteen pieces of silver and ten bushels of barley," cried the relieved auctioneer as he pounded the gavel on the podium. He didn't even ask for any more bids but seemed to quickly announce that Hosea was the successful bidder as if he was afraid he might change his mind.

Ignoring anything else that his neighbors might have to say, Hosea proceeded toward the front to secure his purchase. He left the money and barley with the receiver of bids and started toward Gomer. Her head was still bowed. As much as she wanted to do so, her shame kept forbidding her from lifting her head to see who her buyer was. Then she heard his voice. The one who purchased her was now speaking to her .

"Gomer," he said. As she finally lifted her head, she could see the only man who ever seemed to care for her. He was the only man who ever said, "I love you," to her or showed her any love. He had been her husband and yet she had forsaken and rebelled against his love, bring him shame and pain. Despite all of this, he was willing to have her back. More than that, he was willing to pay to have her back.

Hosea walked forward and removed the fetters from her wrists. He then took the robe that he had brought from home, and threw it over her head. It slid down over her shoulders, covering her entire body. Her shameful, semi-nakedness was now shielded from further exposure.

Hosea ached to take her into his arms right then and there, but he refrained from doing so. "Follow me," was all he said. They started through the crowd and headed for home. Gomer obediently complied with his command.

Voices could be heard as they walked out of the gathering of people. Unfriendly voices they were, but Hosea ignored them all. "He's so stupid. No woman is ever going to make such a fool out of me. She's worthless, nobody else would want her." On and on they railed against him as well as her. The whole crowd seemed to concur that she was garbage and he was a fool.

Hosea couldn't even hear them. He had already heard the voice of Jehovah and was committed to it. As they walked silently on, Hosea mused how fortunate he was to be a symbol of Jehovah. If only his people would come back to him, He would be as happy as Hosea was this day. Yes, his people had rebelled against His love, bringing Him shame, as Gomer had done to Hosea. God's returning people would be to Him, what Gomer was to Hosea, The Apple of his Eye.

CHAPTER EIGHTEEN

"Mommy's home," Ammi rushed into the kitchen to tell his sister. She stood at the sink doing dishes. Her brother's words froze her in place. "Come on, Rahumah, Mommy just came home with Dad." The two rushed into the living room and there she was. After all these years, Mommy had come home at last.

Gomer's heart leapt at the sight of her almost grown up children but still she said nothing. All during the long walk home she kept pondering what her fate might be. She had once been Hosea's wife, but now she was his slave. What does that mean for her? What would her new relationship with him be like? She wasn't sure what the answers to those questions were. She was grateful that he rescued her from what might have been, but she wasn't certain what her new relationship would be.

"Dad," Rahumah asked, "how did you get Mom to come home?"

Unwilling to give all the sordid details to their daughter, he answered, "I paid for her release."

"Why didn't you do that before?" chimed in Ammi.

"She had to be willing for me to do it or I couldn't," he replied in half- truth.

Gomer decided to help her husband out by saying, "The truth is Rahumah, I was being sold as a slave. Your father bought me from the slave market." Those were the first words Gomer had spoken since the purchase had been made. "Now I'm his slave," she muttered in an effort to keep from crying.

"No you're not," retorted Hosea. "You are never to call me 'Master.' That is something I will never be to you. I want you to call me the only thing I ever wanted to be to you. I want you to call me, 'Husband'."

"After everything I did, you still want me to be your wife?"

"Yes, but I'll never force you, like I would if you were my slave. I set you free from slavery and you are free to walk out that door just like you did before. I will never be a slave master to you."

"But how…why, why are you doing this?"

"Before you do leave, if you do, I wanted you to know how much I love you." This remark silenced her. She didn't know what to say. Was it possible that a person could love someone who had treated him so terrible?

"You aren't going to leave, are you Mommy," asked Ammi. The innocence and sincerity of his question broke her heart.

At first she silently shook her head and then replied, "Never again."

"Then you will be my wife," Hosea announced. "You will be the lady of the house and the mother of these children. I give back to you all the rights and privileges you had before you left. It will be as if you never went away."

Once again, as she had several times this day, Gomer was at a loss for words. What a day this had been. She started out groveling in the very dust of humiliation. Now here she was a man's wife, a mother and the lady of a house. She was overwhelmed with amazement. Only Hosea would do a thing like this, only a prophet of Jehovah. Only a God like Jehovah could give a man this much love for a woman because only He had that much love to give.

Ammi could wait no longer. He rushed into his mother's arms. In a few seconds, Rahumah followed suit. For the first time in many years, they had a mother. Not just any mother, their mother.

Gomer held them and stroked them. They felt so very good in her arms. "My children, my children," she cried, "How could I have been so foolish as to leave you?" They held onto each other for a long time. All three hated to let go.

Just then the front door flew open and in came Jezreel. He stopped in his tracks and stared at the scene that was before him. "So it's true. It's all over town that Dad brought you home. They say he bought you at the slave market and paid some ridiculously high price for you.

Now, here you are." He hugged his mother just briefly and then turned to his father and said, "You are an incredible man." It was the first kind words he had spoken to his father in many years.

The newly reunited family hugged and talked for a long time. The reunion seemed to wash therapeutic waters over them all. All of the hurt, resentment, anger and bitterness just washed away as they all enjoyed one another's company.

Suddenly, there came a knock on the front door. Everyone looked at each other, wondering who that might be. The whole family was present, so it had to be a visitor. "I'll get it," said Rahumah. It was obvious that she was accustomed to handling such matters at that home.

"Does a man named Hosea live here?" the female visitor enquired. Gomer heard the voice from the living room. She perked up with wonderment.

"I know that voice," she said. "But it can't be..." leaving the sentence hanging in mid-air, she rushed toward the kitchen door. Both of the women knew each other and they stared at each other in amazement. "I can't believe it. How did you get here?"

"Gomer, I was going to ask you the same thing. How can this be? I'm still in shock."

Turning toward her family, Gomer proudly announced, "Everyone, this is my friend, Rachel." Turning back to her friend she asked, "I never thought I'd see you again and now, here you are. How did this happen?"

"I'm just as shocked to see you, Gomer." They both stopped talking and hugged each other as the tears flowed freely. Finally, they stopped hugging and all sat down, anxious to hear Rachel's story.

"I really never thought I would see you again," said Gomer.

"You probably would not have, except the most amazing thing happened. I still can't believe it. It is just so ...amazing."

"Okay," replied Gomer, "we've established the fact that it was amazing, now what was it? What happened?"

"Well, If you will stop talking, I can tell you." Everyone shared a good laugh about this remark. Gomer didn't realize how good it could feel, just to laugh. After such heavy emotions the laughter seemed like a healing balm applied to her soul. Rachel felt the same way.

Rachel continued, "We were walking through the woods, going to whatever my place of punishment was. I kept ranting about the foolishness of worshipping Baal and how everyone, even the guards had better start worshipping Jehovah. I even told the guards," she said with a smile."

"I bet they liked that," commented Gomer sarcastically.

"Wait a minute," interjected Hosea, "what made you start worshipping Jehovah?"

"Well," answered Rachel, "you did. That day, long ago when you came to the temple and told everyone to turn from Baal and back to Jehovah. You said that he would accept us and love us. A number of Baal's girls eventually turned to Jehovah because of you."

"Wow, that's a shock. I didn't think anyone ever listened to me," Hosea confessed. "It's good to know that someone did."

"Well, what you said proved to be true in my life. As Gomer knows, they were taking me to the worst place. It's a place where people don't live long. As we were going through the woods, a pack of wolves came out of the bushes and started to attack us. Everyone else ran. I just stood there and called out to Jehovah."

"Then what happened?" Gomer anxiously enquired.

"The wolves all ran around me and chased the men."

"I didn't know wolves were so selective," joked Gomer.

"These ones were," answered Rachel. "So I climbed a tree before they could return. They came back and sniffed around for a few minutes and just left. After a long time, I climbed down, wandered in the woods for a few days, eating apples and berries. When no one came to get me, I came here."

"Everyone probably thinks that the wolves got you," Hosea mentioned.

Rachel went on, "So I figure, Jehovah gave me a new lease on life so I came here. I don't know what I'm going to do. I just need some time to figure it out."

"Well you can stay with us until you do figure it out," said Hosea.

"She can stay in my old room," offered Jezreel. "I like farming and I still want to learn the business."

So it was agreed that Rachel would live with them until she found out what Jehovah had in mind for her new lease on life. Rachel was just as amazed with Gomer's story as Gomer was with hers. She turned to Hosea and said, "You are an incredible man."

"That's what I told him," added Jezreel.

"Well, I would say, that Jehovah is an incredible God," added Hosea.

"I would say so too," contributed Rachel. "Gomer, just a few hours ago our lives looked hopeless and now look. Here we are, free from slavery. I think that Hosea is right about what he said about when he told us about Jehovah."

"I'm beginning to see that Hosea was right about a lot of things," Gomer confessed. "I still can't believe that you loved me enough to pay the price to redeem me from slavery after all that I did and the hurtful things I said to you. To steal my friend, Rachel's word, it's … amazing.

"Years ago, Jehovah told me to marry a woman like you. I chose you. I wanted no other. Then a short time ago he told me to again show you my love. I wanted to, but I didn't know how. I couldn't find you. You were gone. Then, thanks to Jehovah I found you and I got there in time to set you free."

Unable to contain herself any longer, Gomer rushed over and caught Hosea up in a strong embrace. "I will always love you, Hosea," she said, "because you loved me first and you loved me long after anyone else would have. My father told me how you supported me even when I was at the temple, when I thought the temple people were doing it. Even while suffering the pain I caused you, you loved me."

Hosea countered, "Remember I told you that Jehovah wanted our marriage to symbolize the relationship Jehovah's relationship with his rebellious people. He loves them no matter how rebellious they are and He would pay any price to gain them back."

"Well, you certainly fulfilled that," conceded Gomer. "Nobody, not even Jehovah Himself could have loved me more. People told me that I didn't really know you and I guess it was true. There is no one on this earth that is more like Jehovah, than you. I'm very happy that you again want me to be your wife, but I would have been anything you want. I'd be your servant, your slave, anything."

"I'm going to spend the rest of my life telling this story," promised Rachel. "A story about a man who was so much like Jehovah that he loved a woman. This woman left him, bringing him pain and shame. Her decision eventually reduced her to being sold into slavery. Yet this man loved her still so much that he paid the price to purchase her and refused to own her as his slave. He made her his wife again."

Hosea added, "Don't forget to say that it is not just the story of my love for Gomer but God's love for all people. The whole point of everything that has happened would be missed if you forget to tell them that."

Rachel looked up and said "If I ever start to doubt that God loves me, I'll just think of your love for Gomer and then I'll be sure that He surely loves me."

"No matter what you may do or how bad you become," added Gomer. "His love for you will never fail. Believe me, I know."

"I know you do," conceded Rachel. "Everyone needs to hear about this. Even when we are unlovely and maybe even unlovable, God still loves us. Hosea showed us that. It's the greatest story anyone could ever tell. It is a love story and I'm going to tell it wherever I go.

PRIMARY SCRIPTURES USED IN HOSEA AND GOMER

HOSEA 2:15- And I will give her vineyards from thence, and the valley of Achor (trouble) for a door of hope.

HOSEA 2:16- And it shall be at that day, saith the Lord, that thou shalt call me Ishi (my husband), and thou shalt call me no more, Baali (lord and master).

HOSEA 2:19- And I will betroth thee unto me for ever; yea I will betroth thee unto me in righterousness, and in judgment, and in lovingkindness and in mercies.

HOSEA 4:1- Hear the word of the Lord, ye children of Israel: for the Lord hath a controversy with the inhabitants of the land, because there is no truth, nor mercy, nor knowledge of God in the land.

HOSEA 4:6- My people are destroyed for lack of knowledge: because thou hast rejected knowledge, I will reject thee…

HOSEA 4:16- For Israel slideth back as a backslidden heifer…

HOSEA 6:1- Come let us return unto the Lord: for he hath torn, and he will heal us; he hath smitten, and he will bind us up.

HOSEA 6:3- Then shall we know, if we follow on to know the Lord…

HOSEA 7:8- Ephraim, he hath mixed himself among the people; Ephraim is a cake not turned.

HOSEA 7:11- Ephraim is also like a silly dove, without heart…

HOSEA 8:14- For Israel hath forgotten his Maker…

HOSEA 14:1- O Israel, return unto the Lord thy God…

HOSEA 14:4- I will heal their backsliding, I will love them freely: for mine anger is turned away from him.

PROVERBS 14:12- There is a way which seemeth right unto man, but the end thereof are the ways of death.

JOHN 15:13- Greater love hath no man than this, that a man lay down his life for his friends.

Would you like to see your manuscript become a book?

If you are interested in becoming a PublishAmerica author, please submit your manuscript for possible publication to us at:

acquisitions@publishamerica.com

You may also mail in your manuscript to:

**PublishAmerica
PO Box 151
Frederick, MD 21705**

We also offer free graphics for Children's Picture Books!

---

www.publishamerica.com

CPSIA information can be obtained at www.ICGtesting.com
Printed in the USA
BVOW082004250712

296200BV00001B/4/P